The Orphan
Ho

©2023 by Molly Britton

Contents

Chapter One

Chapter Two

Chapter Three

Chapter Four

Chapter Five

Chapter Six

Chapter Seven

Chapter Eight

Chapter Nine

Chapter Ten

Chapter Eleven

Chapter Twelve

Chapter Thirteen

Chapter Fourteen

Chapter Fifteen

Chapter Sixteen

Chapter Seventeen

Chapter Eighteen

Epilogue

Chapter One

London, 1855

The sun was just starting to rise when six-year-old Emma woke up at the St. Agnes Orphanage. The harsh voice of Sister Agatha filled the room. "Quickly, girls! There's no time to dawdle," she said, her eyes glaring at a girl who was taking too long to get up.

Emma, who was still lying in her bed, watched the morning unfold. She shared her bed with many other girls in a big room. The morning was a quiet, almost silent time. Only hushed whispers filled the room as the girls got dressed and helped each other with tough laces or lost hairpins.

Shivering slightly from the cold, Emma got up from her bed, wanting to avoid Sister Agatha's anger. Her feet felt the chill of the stone floor. She put on her simple dress, its rough material scratching her skin a bit. She was used to it. She then tied her curly blonde hair into a neat braid.

She didn't pay much attention to the others, or to Sister Agatha. Instead, she let her mind wander. She dreamt of a life outside the orphanage. A life filled with love, warmth, and freedom.

Once she was dressed, Emma paused to look out of the tiny window by her bed. The sun was now up, painting the sky with beautiful shades of pink and orange. It was a sight that gave her hope every day. It reminded her that there was a world out there, waiting for her.

Though she was quiet and small, Emma was also tough and full of dreams. She believed that there was more to life than the orphanage. She hoped that one day, she could live a life she loved.

Once they were all dressed, the girls walked down the narrow staircase to the dining room. It was a big room with long tables and benches. The boys, who had been sleeping in different rooms, joined them there. In total, there were five rooms of children in the orphanage, three for boys and two for girls.

Emma sat down on a bench by herself. It was breakfast time, and all the children sat together, but Emma always ate alone. She preferred it that way. She liked to have a little time to herself, to think and dream.

As she was eating her porridge, a girl she didn't recognise came over to her. The girl had a friendly smile on her face. *She must be new*, Emma thought. The girl sat down next to Emma.

"Hello, my name's Lily. I just arrived yesterday. What's your name?"

Emma paused for a moment. It was rare for anyone to talk to her during mealtime. She looked at the girl and said softly, "I'm Emma."

Lily's smile widened. "Nice to meet you, Emma. I was wondering, do you know where we go after breakfast?"

Emma gave her a small smile back and pointed to the door at the end of the room.

"After breakfast, we go to the classroom. Sister Agatha will show you."

"Thank you, Emma," Lily said, her voice full of gratitude. "Would you mind if I sit with you during lessons?"

The hopeful look on Lily's face made Emma pause. She was about to say yes, but she stopped herself. She had been at the orphanage for as long as she could remember, and she had seen children come and go all the time. She was always the one who stayed. She didn't want to get attached to anyone, only to see them leave.

"Actually, Lily," Emma said, her voice quiet, "It might be better if you found somewhere else to sit during lessons."

The smile on Lily's face faded and she looked disappointed. "Oh, I see," she said, her voice small. "I'm sorry, Emma. I didn't mean to bother you."

Emma felt a pang of guilt as she watched Lily's bright eyes fill with sadness. But she quickly reminded herself that this was for the best. It was easier not to get close to anyone. That way, she wouldn't feel the pain when they left.

"No, Lily, you didn't bother me," Emma said, trying to reassure her. "It's just... people often leave here. I don't want to...," she paused, not quite sure how to explain it without sounding cold. "It's just better if I keep to myself."

Lily nodded, seeming to understand, but her eyes were downcast as she picked up her spoon and focused on her porridge.

Emma felt a twinge of regret. Lily seemed like a nice girl. Emma had learned from experience that it was best not to get attached. After all, she was the only constant in this ever-changing world of the orphanage.

Emma finished her breakfast in silence, her mind filled with thoughts. She was used to the quiet, to the solitude. Today, it felt a little more lonely than usual. As she looked around at the other children, chatting and laughing, she couldn't help but wonder if she was missing out on something. She quickly brushed that thought away. This was her life, and she had to protect her heart.

And yet, as she left the dining room and walked to the classroom, she couldn't help but glance back at Lily. She saw the girl's bright smile return as she talked to a group of other girls. Emma felt a strange pang in her chest. Was it regret? Or perhaps longing? Either way, she pushed the feelings down. This was her choice, and she would stand by it.

After all, she had always been alone. That was what she was used to. That was what was safe. At least, that's what she believed.

As Emma walked into the classroom, she was greeted by the familiar sight of the stern-faced nuns standing at the front. They were always there, ensuring the children received their education, but there was a coldness to their presence that couldn't be ignored.

Sister Agatha, with her constant frown and sharp eyes, led the morning prayers. Her voice echoed in the room, the words as impersonal as they were repetitive. Once the prayers were over, they moved onto their lessons for the day.

The classroom was filled with the sounds of recitation, the nuns correcting the children with a strictness that was almost unkind. They did their duty, teaching the children to read and write, but there was no warmth or love in their teachings. It was clear they viewed it as a job, not a passion.

Emma sat at her desk, her fingers tracing over the letters in her textbook. She did her best to concentrate, to drown out the harsh words of the nuns, but it was hard. The classroom was filled with an air of sternness, a feeling of cold authority that made it difficult to find joy in learning.

She stole a glance at Lily, who was sitting at a desk near the front. The new girl was trying her best to keep up, her eyes wide as she took in the strict teaching style of the nuns. Emma felt a pang of sympathy for her. She had been there once, new and confused. By now, she was used to it.

The day went on, the nuns never smiling, never showing any sign of affection towards the children. The strictness of their behaviour was all too familiar to Emma. It was a constant reminder that this was not a home. It was an institution.

Emma was unhappy. Despite the roof over her head and the food on her plate, she felt an aching emptiness in her heart. She longed for a warmth that seemed out of reach. She longed for someone who would look at her not as a burden, but as a child deserving of love.

The nuns were all she had ever known. Their stern faces and cold words were as much a part of her life as the stone walls of the orphanage. But Emma yearned for more. She yearned for a life beyond the harsh reality of the orphanage.

Every day, she woke up, hoping that the day would bring change. Hoping that something, anything, would be different. Every day, she was met with the same stern faces, the same cold words. It was a cycle of hope and disappointment, a cycle she was desperate to break.

Chapter Two

After classes ended, Emma was tidying her books when Sister Agatha called her name. Her heart thumped hard against her chest as she looked up to see the stern nun standing there, her gaze fixed on Emma.

"Emma, Sister Teresa wishes to see you in her office," she said, her voice as strict as ever.

Fear curled in Emma's stomach. Children were only called into Sister Teresa's office if something significant had happened. "Did I do something wrong, Sister?" she asked, her voice trembling slightly.

Sister Agatha shrugged her shoulders. "I don't know, child. Just follow me."

As they walked through the echoing hallways of the orphanage, Emma felt a knot of anxiety tighten in her stomach. Her mind raced with all the possible reasons she could be summoned.

When they finally reached Sister Teresa's office, the head nun looked up from her desk, her face unreadable. "Sit, child," she said, gesturing to a chair in front of her desk.

Taking a deep breath, Emma did as she was told, her hands folded neatly in her lap.

"I have news for you, Emma," Sister Teresa began, her voice neither warm nor cold. "You have been chosen by a family."

Emma blinked, her heart pounding in her ears. "A family?" she repeated, not quite believing what she was hearing.

"Yes," Sister Teresa continued. "Owen and Abigail Shaw have chosen you. They have no children of their own, and wish to provide a home for a child in need."

Emma felt a wave of emotions crash over her. Fear, confusion, but most of all, an unfamiliar flutter of hope. She had been chosen. After all these years of being alone, of feeling like she was nothing more than a burden, she had been chosen.

"I... I see," Emma managed to say, her voice barely above a whisper. She couldn't quite comprehend what was happening.

"You will leave the orphanage in a week. Pack your belongings," Sister Teresa said, already turning her attention back to the papers on her desk.

"Thank you, Sister Teresa," Emma said, her voice shaky. She got up from her seat, her legs feeling like jelly.

She left the office in a daze, her mind a whirlwind of thoughts. She was leaving the orphanage, going to a family. She was scared, of course, but deep down, she felt a glimmer of hope, a glimmer she hadn't felt in a long time.

Emma followed Sister Agatha out of the office, her mind still spinning from the news. She was led to the kitchen where her daily chores awaited her – washing dishes. As she rolled up her sleeves and prepared to begin, she was surprised to see Lily already there, along with two other girls on the roster.

"Emma!" Lily called out, her face brightening at the sight of her. "I didn't expect to see you here. What did Sister Teresa want?"

Emma paused, her hands hovering over the pile of dirty dishes. "She told me that I've been chosen by a family," she admitted, her voice quiet.

Lily's eyes widened in surprise. "Really? Oh, Emma, that's... that's wonderful!"

Emma shrugged, her feelings still a jumbled mess. "I suppose," she said, her voice unsure. "I mean, it's what we all want, isn't it? To be chosen, to have a family; but it's... it's a lot to take in."

She began washing the dishes, her hands mechanically moving as she spoke.

Lily watched her, her own hands paused in her work.

"I can only imagine," Lily said softly. "It must be scary, but it's also exciting, right? A new start, a new family."

Emma didn't respond for a moment, her mind going over the news again and again. Finally, she sighed, her shoulders dropping slightly. "I don't know, Lily. I just don't know what to make of it all."

Lily gave her a sympathetic look, her hand reaching out to give Emma's a reassuring squeeze. "Whatever happens, Emma," she said gently. "Remember that it's okay to feel confused. It's okay to feel scared. But it's also okay to hope for something better."

Emma looked at Lily, her blue eyes reflecting a whirlwind of emotions. "I hope you're right, Lily," she said, a whisper of a smile on her lips. "I really hope you're right."

And with that, they returned to their chores, the kitchen filled with the sound of clinking dishes and running water. Emma's heart was a turmoil of emotions, but for the first time in a long time, amongst the confusion and the fear, there was a tiny, stubborn spark of hope.

As Emma scrubbed at a particularly stubborn stain, she tuned in to the conversation happening beside her. The other two girls were speaking in hushed voices, their words barely audible over the sound of the running water.

"Did you hear about Thomas, the boy who was adopted last month?" one of the girls, Alice, asked. Alice was the oldest girl in the orphanage and was known for her knack of storytelling.

Lily's eyes widened. "No, what happened?"

Alice leaned in closer, her voice dropping to a conspiratorial whisper. "I heard he was taken in by a rich family, but they didn't want a son. They wanted a servant."

Emma felt a chill run down her spine as Alice continued, "They made him work from dawn till dusk. He was only given the scraps from their table to eat. When he couldn't work anymore, they returned him."

"I thought families who adopt want to love and care for a child," Lily said, her voice trembling.

Alice shook her head, her eyes dark. "Some do, but not all. Some just want a pretty face to show off to their friends. Once they get bored, they return the child like a discarded toy."

The words hung heavy in the air. Emma felt her heart pound in her chest, her earlier spark of hope dimming. Was that what awaited her? A life of labour, or to be used as a decoration?

"That's not fair," Lily protested. "That's not right."

Alice just shrugged, a grim look on her face. "Life's not fair, Lily. The sooner you learn that, the better."

The conversation ended there, the kitchen falling into an uneasy silence. Emma's mind was reeling, her hands moving automatically through her chores. She was no stranger to hard work, but the thought of being discarded once she was no longer of use was terrifying.

She found herself glancing at Lily. The younger girl looked horrified, her eyes wide and scared. Emma wished she could reassure her, tell her that everything would be okay. She couldn't. Not when she herself was so full of fear and uncertainty.

She finished her chores in silence, the disturbing conversation playing over and over in her mind. The prospect of her upcoming adoption filled her not with hope but with dread. She remembered Lily's words from earlier. It was okay to feel scared. It was okay to feel confused. It was okay to hope.

After their chores, the girls began to head back to their shared rooms, the halls of the orphanage echoing with their hushed chatter. Alice, the ever-present spinner of tales, led the group with an air of superiority.

As they walked, Alice turned to Emma, a smirk playing on her lips. "I wonder how long you'll last, Emma," she said, her tone as cold as ice. "A week? Maybe a month? Or perhaps they'll return you after a day."

Emma faltered, her heart pounding. Alice's words, though cruel, echoed her own fears. She forced herself to keep walking, to not let Alice see how much her words had hurt.

"Emma is smart and kind," Lily defended, her voice full of conviction. "Any family would be lucky to have her."

Alice just laughed, the sound echoing off the cold stone walls. "Kindness and smarts won't make them keep her, Lily. They'll tire of her just like they do with the others."

The rest of their walk back to their room was spent in silence, Alice's words hanging heavy in the air. Emma felt her heart grow heavier with each step she took. Could Alice be right? Would she be returned once her new family grew bored of her?

As she climbed into her bed that night, Emma found herself staring at the ceiling, her mind filled with worries. She wished she could believe Lily, wished she could believe that everything would be okay. But Alice's words were like a poison, slowly seeping into her thoughts and filling her with dread.

Emma knew she should be excited about her upcoming adoption. It was what she had always wanted, after all. Yet, as she lay in the dark, the echoes of Alice's cruel laughter ringing in her ears, she couldn't help but feel a deep, gnawing fear.

She was about to step into the unknown. And though she hoped for the best, she couldn't shake off the worry that Alice might be right.

Chapter Three

A week later, Emma found herself standing nervously in Sister Teresa's office, her small bag of belongings clutched tightly in her hand. Today was the day. Today she would meet her new parents.

The door opened, and in walked a woman with a warm smile and a man with a quiet, gentle presence. "Emma," Sister Teresa introduced, "this is Abigail and Owen Shaw."

Abigail immediately came over to her, her eyes shining with kindness. "Hello, Emma," she said, her voice bubbling with enthusiasm. "We're so happy to finally meet you."

Owen nodded, a small smile on his face. "Indeed, we are," he added, his voice deep and soothing.

They took her to a carriage waiting outside the orphanage. As they travelled, Abigail filled the silence with her cheery chatter. She spoke of their home, of the room they had prepared for Emma, and of the small town they lived in.

Emma listened quietly, her gaze fixed on the passing scenery outside the carriage window. She wanted to believe Abigail's words, wanted to believe that this could be her new beginning. But she couldn't shake off her fear. She remembered Alice's words, remembered the cruel laughter. She was terrified that this, too, could end in disappointment.

"Are you all right, Emma?" Abigail asked, breaking into her thoughts.

Emma forced a small smile. "Yes, thank you, Mrs Shaw," she replied, her voice barely above a whisper.

Abigail smiled back, reaching out to squeeze Emma's hand. "Just Abigail, dear," she said. "You're part of our family now."

Emma nodded, her heart pounding. Family. The word felt foreign on her tongue, but she tried to hold onto it. To hope that maybe, just maybe, things could turn out all right.

As the carriage rumbled on, Emma looked back at the orphanage disappearing in the distance. She knew she was leaving behind a life of hardship, but it was a life she knew. Now, she was heading into the unknown. Though she was scared, she also felt a small spark of hope kindling in her heart. It was a chance for a new beginning, and Emma, brave and resilient as always, was ready to face it.

The carriage ride seemed to go by in a blur, and before Emma knew it, they were standing in front of a small, cosy house. It was modest, but warm and inviting. Emma's heart pounded in her chest as she stepped inside.

Abigail immediately set about making her feel at home. She showed her the small room that was to be hers, its walls painted a soft blue and a plush bed sitting invitingly in the corner. It was a far cry from the communal dormitory she was used to.

Owen, meanwhile, hung back, his presence a comforting constant. He would chime in occasionally, offering a gentle word or a small smile. Together, they made her feel more welcome than she'd ever felt before.

As the tour continued, Emma found herself beginning to relax. The kind smiles, the gentle words, the cosy rooms – it was all so different from what she had known. She found herself responding to their affection, her guarded walls slowly coming down.

In the kitchen, Abigail showed her where they kept the dishes and how to work the stove. Owen showed her the small garden at the back, his eyes lighting up as he talked about the various plants and vegetables they grew.

Through it all, Emma couldn't help but feel a sense of peace settling over her. She could see the love and care that had gone into every corner of this house. It was clear that the Shaws wanted her to be a part of this, to be a part of their family.

As the day wore on, Emma found herself warming up to her new parents. Their kindness and patience calmed her anxious heart. For the first time in a long time, Emma felt like she could breathe.

When dinner time rolled around, Emma found herself sitting at a small table with Abigail and Owen. In front of her was a simple stew, but the aroma wafting from it was unlike anything she had smelled at the orphanage. The food there was always tasteless and over-boiled; this was a welcome change.

"It's not much," Abigail said, smiling at Emma as she served her a portion. "Still, we hope you like it."

Emma took a tentative bite, and her eyes widened. The flavours were rich and comforting, a far cry from the bland meals she was used to. "It's really good," she admitted, her voice soft.

Over dinner, Abigail and Owen encouraged her to share a bit about herself. It was difficult at first, but their patience and kindness made it easier.

"I was left at the orphanage steps when I was a baby," she admitted, her voice barely a whisper. "I don't remember my real parents."

There was silence for a moment, then Owen spoke, his voice gentle. "Emma, we want you to know that you're part of our family now. We may not share blood, but that doesn't make us any less of a family."

Abigail nodded, her hand reaching out to cover Emma's. "We're here for you, Emma. You're not alone anymore."

The words were a balm to Emma's hurting heart. For so long, she had longed for a family, for a sense of belonging. And though she still felt a pang of loss for the parents she never knew, she found herself feeling hopeful.

As they finished dinner and cleaned up together, Emma found herself feeling lighter. The Shaws, with their kindness and understanding, had managed to ease some of her fears. She wasn't just a stranger in their home; she was family.

As she climbed into bed that night, Emma found herself smiling for the first time in a long while. Her heart still held fears and uncertainties, but there was also hope.

She was home. Not in a crowded dormitory in a cold orphanage, but in a warm, welcoming house with people who cared about her. It was a new start, and Emma found herself looking forward to what was to come.

Chapter Four

Christmas arrived with a flurry of snow and the scent of baking in the air. Emma found herself in the kitchen with Abigail, both of them covered in flour as they baked cookies and prepared the Christmas dinner. It was a far cry from the meagre, joyless Christmases she had spent at the orphanage.

Back at the orphanage, they had a tree, but there were no presents to be found under it, no special dinner to look forward to. Here, the house was filled with laughter and warmth, the air humming with anticipation.

As they laid out the food on the table, Owen disappeared for a moment. When he returned, he held a small package in his hands. "A little something for you, Emma," he said, a twinkle in his eyes as he handed her the gift.

Emma unwrapped it carefully, her heart pounding. Inside was a small, handmade wooden toy set. The craftsmanship was exquisite, and it was clear that a lot of thought and care had gone into making it. "I made it myself," Owen confessed, looking a bit embarrassed. "I thought you might like it."

Emma felt tears pricking at her eyes. "It's beautiful," she whispered, tracing her fingers over the small figures. "Thank you, Owen."

In response, she reached into her pocket and pulled out two small, homemade Christmas ornaments. "I made these," she said shyly, handing one to each of them. "They're not much, but..."

"They're perfect," Abigail cut in, her eyes glistening as she looked at the ornament. "Thank you, Emma. This means a lot to us."

That Christmas, they ate, laughed, and shared stories around the table. Emma had never felt such warmth, such joy. She had spent so many years longing for a family, and now she had one.

After dinner, as Emma helped Owen clear the table and wash the dishes, the house was filled with the soft sounds of laughter and chatter. The warmth of the family conversation was a far cry from the cold silences she had known at the orphanage.

"Did you enjoy your first Christmas here, Emma?" Owen asked, a kind smile on his face as he dried a plate.

"Yes," she replied, a small smile tugging at her lips. "It's the best Christmas I've ever had. Thank you."

Owen looked at her warmly, ruffling her blonde curls gently. "We're happy you're here with us, Emma."

As they finished cleaning up, Owen broached a new topic. "We usually visit some extended family for New Year's," he explained. "They're all quite excited to meet you. Would you like that?"

The idea of meeting more family was both thrilling and nerve-wracking. But remembering the warmth and kindness she had received from Abigail and Owen, she felt more excitement than fear.

"Yes, I'd love to meet them," Emma said, her voice barely more than a whisper.

"Great!" Owen said, his green eyes twinkling with anticipation. "They're going to love you, Emma."

For the first time, she felt a sense of belonging. She wasn't just an orphan anymore; she was part of a family. As she dried the last plate and put it away, a sense of contentment settled over her.

Abigail joined them in the kitchen just as they finished tidying up, a warm smile on her face. "You two have done a wonderful job," she praised, looking around the sparkling clean kitchen.

She then turned to Emma, her blue eyes soft with affection. "We're so glad you're here, Emma. You've made this Christmas extra special."

Emma looked at her, surprised. "Me?"

"Yes, you," Abigail confirmed with a nod. "You've brought so much joy into our lives, dear. And we can't wait for you to meet the rest of the family. You've got aunts and uncles, cousins... and they're all so excited to meet you."

The idea of having such a large family was still new and overwhelming to Emma, but it was also incredibly exciting. She had always yearned for a sense of belonging, and now it felt like she was finally getting it.

"You know," Owen added, looking at Emma, "Abigail and I... we were never able to have children of our own, but we've always wanted a family."

Abigail nodded, her hand reaching out to cover Emma's. "We're so happy to call you our daughter, Emma."

The words hit Emma like a wave, overwhelming her with a rush of emotions. She was their daughter. She had a family. The reality of it made her eyes well up with tears.

"Oh, don't cry, love," Abigail said, pulling Emma into a comforting hug. "These are happy tears, aren't they?"

Emma nodded, unable to speak. She was overcome with the love she felt from Owen and Abigail. It was a feeling she hadn't known before, but now couldn't imagine being without.

As they shared that moment, the house around them quiet and peaceful, Emma felt a warmth spread through her heart. This was what family felt like. This was what love felt like. This was what home felt like.

As she went to bed that night, she couldn't help but feel a sense of pure, unabridged joy. She was Emma Shaw now. She had a family that loved her, and she loved them.

She was home, and she was happy. For the first time in her life, Emma went to sleep with a smile on her face, her heart filled with hope and happiness, excited for all the days to come.

Chapter Five

Six years later

Six years had passed since Emma's first Christmas with the Shaws, and each year the holiday season brought with it a new wave of joy and warmth. Now, as a twelve-year-old, Emma eagerly anticipated the coming festivities. The scent of fresh pine and the sound of carols filled the house, creating an atmosphere of cheery anticipation.

She was hanging ornaments on the tree, her fingers gently placing each delicate decoration, while Abigail lit the candles that were nestled between the pine boughs on the mantelpiece. Owen was outside, shovelling the recent snowfall from the front path. Their home felt like a scene from a Christmas card, full of love and holiday spirit.

Suddenly, an ear-piercing scream shattered the peace. Emma turned towards the sound in time to see Abigail backing away from the fireplace, her face white with fear. "Fire!" she cried, stumbling over her own feet in an effort to get away.

Thick black smoke began to billow from the mantelpiece. The flames, once small and contained within the candles, had somehow reached the pine boughs and begun to spread rapidly.

Before Emma could fully comprehend what was happening, the fire had engulfed the room. She could see the bright, terrifying flames under the door, consuming the beautiful Christmas decorations and transforming their peaceful home into a scene of chaos.

Just then, the front door burst open and Owen rushed in. His face was pale, his eyes wide with fear. He spotted Emma and quickly made his way towards her, pushing past the growing flames and smoke.

"Emma!" he shouted, grabbing her hand and pulling her towards him. His grip was firm, his eyes filled with determination. "We need to get out!"

With that, he led her through the smoke and flames, his strong arm around her small frame providing a semblance of safety amidst the chaos. The heat was intense, the smoke suffocating, but Owen didn't let go. He kept moving, guiding them towards the front door and away from the inferno.

Emma looked back, trying to spot Abigail. A wall of fire now separated them, the flames too high and intense to pass through. Her heart pounded in her chest as she called out for Abigail, but her voice was drowned out by the crackling of the fire.

Just as they made it to the entrance, a loud, gut-wrenching crack echoed through the house. Emma looked back just in time to see the wooden beam above the fireplace collapse, sending a shower of sparks and flames across the room.

They tumbled out into the snowy yard, the icy air a harsh contrast to the sweltering heat they'd just escaped. Emma turned back to see their once beautiful home now an engulfed inferno, the flames reaching high into the night sky. Their Christmas, their home, had been consumed by the fire.

She was safe. Owen was safe. And as she looked at him, his face streaked with soot but unharmed, she felt an overwhelming sense of relief. But where was Abigail? The reality of the situation crashed into Emma, and her heart filled with dread.

Owen looked back at Emma, his eyes meeting hers with an intensity that terrified her. "Stay here," he commanded, his voice filled with a deadly calm. Before she could respond, he turned and plunged back into the burning house, disappearing into the thick smoke.

Emma tried to follow him, her heart screaming for her to help. But strong hands grabbed her, pulling her back. It was the

Thompsons from next door, their faces pale with fear.

"Let me go!" Emma cried, trying to wiggle free from their hold. "I need to help them!"

"Emma, dear, you can't," Mrs Thompson said, her voice shaking. "It's too dangerous."

"My parents are in there!" Emma sobbed, pointing towards the house. The flames had consumed nearly all of it now, the fire eating away at their happy home. All she could think about was Owen and Abigail, trapped inside.

Minutes stretched into what felt like hours as Emma watched in helpless terror, waiting for Owen to reappear. She could hear the distant sound of people shouting, the clatter of buckets, as the neighbours began to form a line to pass water from the nearby well to the fire.

It was too late. The house was fully ablaze, the fire too hot and fierce to be quelled by mere buckets of water. The reality of the situation began to set in. They were not coming out.

"No," Emma whispered, her voice barely audible above the chaos. "No, this can't be happening."

Mrs Thompson pulled her into a tight embrace, her own tears falling onto Emma's golden curls. "I'm so sorry, dear," she whispered, her voice choked with emotion. "I'm so, so sorry."

Emma stood there, in the arms of her neighbour, as her world crumbled around her. The glow from the fire illuminated her tear-streaked face, reflecting in her wide, horrified blue eyes. The sounds of the fire and the panicked shouts of the villagers were a distant hum, drowned out by the deafening silence in her own mind.

The fire roared on, relentless and merciless, claiming the lives of those Emma loved most. Her joyous Christmas morning had turned into a nightmarish scene. She was alone, once again, her newly found happiness ripped away as quickly as it had come. Her heart felt heavy in her chest, the reality of the situation too painful to comprehend. The last thing she saw before collapsing into Mrs Thompson's arms was the silhouette of their beloved house, now nothing more than a glowing skeleton in the cold winter night.

Emma's sobs filled the cold night air, echoing eerily against the backdrop of the crackling fire. The tears fell freely now, hot and unending, tracing wet paths down her dirt-streaked face. Her heart pounded painfully in her chest, each beat a stark reminder of the horror unfolding before her eyes.

She shook violently in Mrs Thompson's arms, the woman's attempts to soothe her having little effect on her uncontrollable sobbing. Each breath was a struggle, her lungs heavy with smoke and grief. Her mind spun with a maelstrom of fear and sorrow, unable to process the magnitude of her loss.

Mrs Thompson held Emma close, whispering comforting words into her ear as her own tears fell. "Shh, Emma dear, it's okay," she cooed, her hands rubbing small circles on Emma's back. Her words felt hollow, the reassurances doing nothing to quell the despair clawing at Emma's heart.

As the hours passed, the ferocious flames that had consumed the house began to die down. The villagers, their faces sombre and weary, continued to douse the smouldering ruins with water. The once vibrant home was now nothing but a charred, smoking husk, a chilling reminder of the tragedy that had occurred.

Emma couldn't tear her eyes away. The sight was horrifying, yet she was entranced, her gaze locked on the remnants of her shattered life. She felt a numbing cold seep into her bones, the winter chill nothing compared to the icy dread that filled her heart.

Even as the sky began to lighten with the approach of dawn, Emma remained motionless, her eyes never leaving the smouldering ruins. She clung to Mrs Thompson, her small frame trembling with the force of her sobs. The reality of her loss was slowly sinking in, each passing moment a harsh reminder of her newfound loneliness.

Emma's heart ached with a depth of sorrow she had never known. A profound emptiness filled her, the place where Owen and Abigail had resided in her heart now void. They had been her family, her refuge, the ones who had pulled her from a life of loneliness and showed her love. Now, they were gone.

She could no longer contain the heart-wrenching sobs that wracked her body. She cried for her loss, for the loving parents she had known for too short a time. She cried for the warmth that was no more, for the laughter and love that had been so cruelly snatched away.

As the dawn broke, casting long shadows over the remnants of the house, Emma wept. She wept for the shattered pieces of her heart, for the love and warmth that had been cruelly ripped away from her. Amidst the cold ashes of her former home, Emma mourned, a lone figure huddled against the harsh reality of her loss.

Chapter Six

Two days after the fire, Emma was standing outside a different home, Uncle Edward's home. It was a modest house, nestled between a bakery and a blacksmith shop. Uncle Edward Turner was Abigail's older brother, a tall man with a stoic face etched with grief.

"Emma," Uncle Edward said, his voice low and sombre as he greeted her at the door. "I'm...I'm sorry for your loss."

Emma nodded, her own grief reflecting in her wide blue eyes. "I'm sorry, too."

Uncle Edward ushered her inside where his three children were waiting, their small faces filled with confusion and curiosity.

Flora, the eldest at nine, was the spitting image of her father. Beatrice, the middle child at six, shared her father's brown eyes. Little Luke, just four years old, looked unsure, clinging to his older sisters.

"Girls, Luke," Edward said, "This is your cousin Emma. She'll be staying with us for a while."

Emma offered them a small smile, her heart aching as she remembered how she'd played with them during family gatherings. They'd always been distant then, a part of a life she'd yearned for but couldn't have. And now, they were her family.

"Hello," Flora said, stepping forward with a shy smile. "It's good to see you, Emma."

Emma's throat tightened, and she nodded, swallowing hard. "It's good to see you too, Flora."

Beatrice, her little brows furrowed, walked up to Emma. "Why are you going to stay with us?" she asked, her innocent question piercing Emma's heart.

Uncle Edward cleared his throat, stepping in before Emma could answer. "Emma's mama and papa...they're gone, Beatrice. She's going to stay with us now because we're family, and family takes care of each other."

Emma felt tears sting her eyes at his words. They were family; but it felt so wrong, not when she'd lost the two people who'd made her feel a part of one. The room fell into an uncomfortable silence, the weight of the situation hanging heavy in the air.

Finally, Luke, still clinging to Flora, broke the silence. "Does this mean Emma can play with us now?" he asked, looking from his father to Emma with wide eyes.

Emma found herself chuckling, despite the tears that were threatening to spill. "Yes, Luke," she said, managing a smile. "Maybe later, though."

***

Over the next few days, Emma found herself gravitating towards Luke. The little boy was too young to comprehend the magnitude of their loss, his innocence a refreshing change from how Beatrice and Flora sent her scathing looks. They spent long hours playing in the small garden, their laughter filling the air, a stark contrast to the solemn atmosphere inside the house.

Flora and Beatrice, however, found it harder to connect with Emma. She seemed like a ghost of the vibrant girl they once knew. They watched from a distance as Emma played with Luke, their own hearts heavy with confusion and sadness.

One evening, Emma found herself alone with Uncle Edward in the sitting room. The girls were upstairs, and Luke had fallen asleep, his little head resting on Emma's lap. Uncle Edward was sitting across from her, his gaze lost in the dancing flames of the fireplace.

"Emma," he said after a long silence, his voice quiet in the room. "I know this isn't easy. For any of us."

Emma looked at him, her eyes mirroring his sadness. "I know, Uncle Edward."

There was another pause before Edward sighed. "I want you to know, I'm... I'm here for you. For all of you. I know I can't replace Owen and Abigail, but I... I'll do my best to care for you."

Emma's heart ached at his words. She knew Uncle Edward was going through his own struggles, having recently lost his wife to another man. He was now left with the responsibility of raising four children, one of whom was a new addition under the most tragic circumstances.

"I know, Uncle Edward," Emma said, giving him a small, appreciative smile. "I'm here for you too."

Edward looked at her, surprise flashing across his features before being replaced by a look of gratitude. "Thank you, Emma. That... that means a lot."

As the night grew darker and the fire in the hearth dimmed, Emma felt a small sense of comfort. She had lost so much, and her heart still ached with the absence of her parents. She wasn't alone. She was with family. It wasn't perfect, and it wasn't what she would've chosen, but for now, it was enough.

In the silence of the room, Emma let herself close her eyes, lulled by the soft crackling of the dying fire. Tomorrow was another day, another step towards healing, towards understanding this new life she was thrust into. For now, in this moment, she had Uncle Edward and her cousins, she had family. And in the heartache and loss, that was something to hold on to.

Chapter Seven

Time passed in Uncle Edward's house. The initial kindness that had enveloped Emma in the wake of her tragedy began to wane. Edward's patience grew thinner, and the house seemed to reflect his mood, the warmth that had once been there slowly draining away.

One morning, as Emma was preparing breakfast, Uncle Edward entered the kitchen. He had a grave look on his face, his eyebrows knit together in a frown.

"Emma," he began, "I need you to take over the household chores while I'm at work."

Emma looked up from the stove, surprised. "All of them, Uncle Edward?"

Edward nodded. "Yes, and look after Flora, Beatrice, and Luke."

Emma's surprise grew into worry. "Oh. Uncle Edward, I... I don't know if I can manage everything."

Edward's frown deepened, and he snapped, "You'll have to learn, Emma. I can't do it all."

"But Uncle Edward," Emma protested, "Flora, Beatrice, and Luke... they need someone who knows how to look after them. I can try, but..."

She was cut off by Edward's curt response, "Then you'll have to learn quickly, won't you?"

Emma fell silent, taken aback by Edward's harshness. The air in the room grew tense, and for a moment, the only sound was the quiet bubbling of the porridge on the stove.

"I... I'll do my best, Uncle Edward," Emma finally said, her voice barely above a whisper. But inside, she was filled with worry. She was no more than a child herself, yet now she was expected to shoulder the responsibilities of a grown woman. Although, she didn't want to let down her cousins, who had been through so much already.

Uncle Edward simply nodded and left the room, leaving Emma standing alone in the kitchen. The feeling of warmth that had slowly begun to build since her arrival had been replaced by a sense of apprehension. Her new home suddenly felt a lot less like home and more like a daunting task waiting to be tackled.

She had no choice. Emma knew she had to step up, for her own sake and for the sake of her younger cousins. So, she steeled herself, finished making breakfast, and promised to do her best, no matter how hard it would be.

At breakfast, Emma's worries transformed into reality. Luke, with his boundless energy, refused to stay put, running around the kitchen while his porridge went cold. Flora and Beatrice, meanwhile, engaged in a relentless battle of bickering that seemed to grow louder with each passing minute.

"Luke, please sit," Emma implored the young boy, but he just giggled and continued his antics. At the same time, she was trying to mediate the escalating argument between Flora and Beatrice.

"Girls, please," she pleaded, her voice nearly drowned out by their bickering.

In her effort to manage everything, her elbow brushed against a plate, sending it crashing to the ground. The noise was deafening, a sharp interruption to the chaos that had filled the kitchen. Everyone went silent, looking at the shards of porcelain scattered across the floor.

"I... I'm sorry," Emma stammered, mortified. She quickly bent down to start picking up the pieces, her face turning red with embarrassment.

"Wait, Emma," Flora's voice sounded. She was already by Emma's side, holding out a hand to stop her. "Let me help."

Emma looked up, surprised to see Flora extending her an olive branch amidst the chaos. The older girl looked determined, a stark contrast to her usual reserved demeanour.

"You've got enough on your plate," Flora said, her voice a lot softer than before.

"But... but Uncle Edward..." Emma began to protest, glancing towards the door, half-expecting Edward to come in any second.

"He won't know," Flora interrupted her, "We can clean this up together, quickly."

In that moment, Emma felt a strange sense of relief. Here was Flora, the girl who had kept her distance ever since Emma's arrival, offering to help. Emma gave her a grateful smile and nodded.

Together, they swept up the broken pieces, managing to clear away the evidence before anyone else could notice. As they worked, they barely spoke, but the silence was not uncomfortable. For the first time, Emma didn't feel completely alone in her struggles.

Once they were done, Flora looked at Emma, a faint smile on her face. "We'll get through this, Emma," she said quietly.

Emma nodded, feeling a surge of warmth for her cousin. "Yes, we will," she echoed, her voice filled with a newfound determination.

***

Emma was in the middle of preparing supper when Uncle Edward walked in. His usually straight posture was slouched, dark circles underscored his tired eyes. He kicked off his boots, leaving muddy footprints on the freshly cleaned wooden floor.

"Emma!" he barked, his voice echoing in the quiet kitchen. Emma flinched at his tone, glancing his way. "You've let Luke make a mess again," he grumbled, pointing at a puddle of water Luke had spilled earlier.

"I...I'm sorry," Emma stammered, "I was about to clean it up." She moved quickly to wipe up the water, her heart pounding in her chest.

Uncle Edward grunted in response, then turned to his children who had come running at the sound of his voice. To them, his tone softened, "Did you have a good day, my dears?"

Flora and Beatrice nodded, their faces lighting up in response to their father's rare display of warmth. Emma watched from the corner of her eye, her heart aching. Why couldn't he be like that with her?

Once the children had scampered off to play, Uncle Edward ascended the stairs, leaving Emma alone in the kitchen. Emma fought back tears, her heart heavy.

Later, in the room they shared, Flora found Emma sitting on the bed, staring into space. Flora took a seat beside her, looking at her cousin with sympathy.

"He's not usually like this, you know," she said softly.

Emma turned to look at her, a glimmer of hope in her eyes. "Really?" she asked.

Flora nodded. "After Mum left, and now...losing Aunt Abigail, he's been different. He used to be a lot nicer. To us and to others," she explained.

Emma looked down, biting her lip. "It's just...he's so kind to you, and Luke, and Beatrice, but...with me..."

"I know," Flora cut her off gently. "Don't take it personally, Emma. He's just...struggling. We all are."

Flora placed a comforting arm around Emma, pulling her into a hug. "We're family, Emma. And we'll stick together, okay?"

Emma nodded, tears welling up in her eyes. For the first time in a long time, she felt like she belonged, even if it was just a tiny bit. For now, that was enough.

***

Emma woke up early the next morning. The sky was still dark, with only a faint glow hinting at the approaching dawn. She slipped out of bed, careful not to disturb the slumbering forms of Flora and Beatrice.

Heading into the kitchen, she began preparing breakfast. Beatrice, who had woken up at the sounds of clattering dishes, soon joined her.

"Can I help?" Beatrice asked, her sleepy voice echoing in the quiet kitchen.

Emma nodded, passing Beatrice a bowl. "Can you mix these eggs, please?"

Beatrice took the bowl eagerly and started to whisk the eggs while Emma worked on the bacon and toast. As they worked, they chatted. Emma found herself laughing at Beatrice's silly stories, the tension of the previous day easing off.

After a while, Beatrice paused, her whisk suspended over the bowl. "Emma?" she asked, her voice serious.

Emma looked at her, a sense of trepidation creeping over her. "Yes, Beatrice?"

"Do you...do you like living here?" Beatrice asked hesitantly.

Emma paused, considering the question. She thought about Uncle Edward, about his harsh words, his tired eyes. Then she thought about Beatrice and Flora, and little Luke.

"I...I appreciate being here," Emma finally answered. "I appreciate that you and Flora, and Luke, have been kind to me."

Beatrice nodded, her eyes serious. "You don't feel happy, do you?"

Emma bit her lip, then shook her head.

Beatrice seemed to consider this for a moment. Then, she put down the whisk and turned to Emma. "You know, Emma, you're not ungrateful for feeling like this."

Emma blinked, surprised at Beatrice's words. "I..."

"No," Beatrice interrupted her gently. "Everyone wants to feel loved and welcomed. You're not ungrateful for wanting that."

Tears welled up in Emma's eyes. She quickly wiped them away, giving Beatrice a small smile. "Thank you, Beatrice."

Beatrice returned her smile, her own eyes shining with unshed tears. "We're family, Emma. Family supports each other, no matter what."

Emma was grateful for Beatrice's help in the kitchen that morning. The young girl proved to be a wonderful assistant, whisking the eggs with care, adding the bacon to the pan at just the right moment, and even managing to toast the bread without burning it.

Their shared laughter echoed throughout the kitchen, a warmth blossoming between them that made Emma's heart feel full. It was an unexpected camaraderie, but one that Emma cherished.

When Flora and Luke joined them at the table, Emma noticed the affectionate smile that Flora sent her way. It was a small gesture, but one that held a lot of meaning. It was a reassurance that Flora, at least, was on her side.

The warm bubble of contentment was shattered when Uncle Edward entered the room. His usual brooding expression was firmly in place, his eyes barely acknowledging Emma's presence. Instead, he focused his attention on the list of chores he expected Emma to complete while he was away on his errands.

Emma bit back a sigh, her hands clenched in her lap under the table. The harsh reality of her situation settled on her like a heavy shroud. It wasn't that she was ungrateful for the roof over her head and the food on her plate, but the lack of warmth from Uncle Edward was a stark contrast to the genuine affection that the Shaw's had showered upon her.

She wanted to speak up, to tell him how she really felt. She wanted to ask why his own children received love and kindness, while she, despite her best efforts, was met with cold indifference. But she held her tongue, not wanting to make a scene. Instead, she nodded, promising to complete the tasks to the best of her ability.

As Uncle Edward left, Emma glanced at Flora and Beatrice, their sympathetic gazes met her own. She tried to offer them a small smile, but she wasn't sure if it reached her eyes. For now, she knew she had to endure. Emma was also a determined young woman, and she made a promise to herself: she wouldn't let Uncle Edward's coldness diminish her spirit.

Chapter Eight

Six years later

Emma navigated the bustling marketplace, her list of ingredients for dinner clutched tightly in her hand. It was a chaotic place, but she had become accustomed to it. However, in her haste, she bumped into a figure causing her to lose her footing slightly.

"I'm so sorry, sir," Emma apologised quickly, stepping back to give the gentleman room.

"No harm done, Miss," the stranger replied, steadying her with a strong hand on her elbow. He was dressed in a smart uniform that was far too lavish for their part of town.

"My name's William," he said, extending a hand towards her. His hair was a messy shade of brown, his skin marked with a smattering of freckles, and he had the most striking green eyes she had ever seen. "William Maxwell."

"Emma," she responded, shaking his hand. The whole time, she had to wonder just why he was bothering to introduce himself to a common girl like herself. "Emma Turner… Shaw."

"What brings a well-dressed footman like you to our humble marketplace, William?" Emma asked, her eyes glancing over his neat attire once more.

He chuckled, his green eyes twinkling in the midday sun. "My master is a generous man, always ensuring we're well turned out.

He believes that how we present ourselves reflects upon him."

Emma nodded, appreciating the honesty in his words. "That's rare," she admitted, "Not many masters care for their servants in such a way."

"Indeed," he agreed, "I am fortunate. I don't mind an excuse to explore different parts of town."

They shared a brief moment of silence before Emma decided to move along, "I best be on my way, William. I've got dinner to sort out."

"A pleasure meeting you, Emma," he said, nodding his head respectfully. "Perhaps we'll run into each other again."

Emma had barely taken two steps when William called after her. "Wait, Miss Emma!" He sounded almost flustered, not at all like the confident man she'd just been speaking to.

She turned back, surprised. "Yes, Mr Maxwell?"

He scratched the back of his neck, his cheeks flushing slightly. "I'm actually not too familiar with this part of town. I... um, I was hoping you could point me in the right direction?"

She cocked her head, puzzled. "Direction for what, exactly?"

"Cufflinks," he admitted, almost sheepishly.

At that, Emma couldn't help but let out a laugh. It echoed through the noise of the marketplace, light and genuine. "Cufflinks? Here? William, this isn't exactly the place for such fineries."

William chuckled, shrugging a bit. "It was worth a shot. You never know where you might find hidden gems."

Emma considered this, her amusement still tugging at the corners of her mouth. "That's true, but I don't think you'll find much in the way of cufflinks here. Most of the people in these parts have little use for them. However," she glanced at a small stall selling various trinkets, "I think I know a place that might just work."

She led him through the bustling market, expertly weaving between the throngs of people. It was a humble place, the kind of stall that only locals knew about. The elderly woman who ran it had an eye for unique items and could spot a valuable trinket from a mile away.

Emma introduced William to the stall owner, explaining his need. The woman chuckled, patting William's hand as she disappeared into the back of her stall. A few moments later, she returned with a small box, containing a pair of intricately designed cufflinks.

Emma watched as William's eyes lit up, clearly impressed with the find. He thanked the stall owner profusely, and turned to Emma with a grateful smile.

"Thank you, Emma," he said, "I don't think I would've found these without your help."

Emma shrugged modestly, "It was nothing, really. Just a bit of local knowledge."

"Local knowledge indeed," William echoed, his smile warm as he secured the small box in his coat pocket. "I should seek your help more often, it seems."

Emma shrugged off his praise, but she couldn't stop the blush from creeping onto her cheeks. "I'm not sure I'd be much help elsewhere. I'm more comfortable with turnips than cufflinks."

William laughed, a hearty sound that seemed to make the whole marketplace brighter. "I don't doubt that, Emma. It's your eye for the uncommon and rare that's truly invaluable."

Emma tilted her head to one side, her eyes narrowing slightly. There was something about William's manner, his careful words, his too-neat clothes, that felt a little off. He certainly didn't seem like any footman she'd ever met.

"Perhaps," she replied slowly, "I can't imagine there's much need for that in your line of work."

His eyes met hers, a touch of amusement in his gaze. "You'd be surprised, Emma. My master is quite... particular."

They shared a moment of easy silence, their playful banter allowing a quiet companionship to settle between them. Emma found herself drawn to William's quick wit and easy-going nature. He was a stark contrast to the usual folk she encountered in her day-to-day life, and she couldn't deny the allure of his difference.

"Well," Emma said, pushing away her curiosity, "I should be off. The Shaws… uh Turners… are probably wondering where I've run off to."

"The Shaws, Turners," William repeated, his expression thoughtful, "Your family?"

"Yes," Emma replied, "In a manner of speaking. They…the Shaws… my parents… there was a fire six years ago and…now I live with my uncle and his family, Edward Turner."

For a moment, she thought she saw something flicker in William's eyes –

sympathy, perhaps, or understanding – but it was gone before she could be sure.

"I should probably head back myself," William said, casting a final glance over the bustling marketplace, "Thank you again, Emma. It was a pleasure meeting you."

"The pleasure was mine, Mr Maxwell," Emma responded, finding that she meant it more than she'd expected.

As she watched him walk away, disappearing into the crowd, Emma couldn't help but feel a strange mix of emotions. Intrigue, excitement, confusion – and, surprisingly, a twinge of disappointment.

With William's words echoing in her mind, Emma meandered her way back home. Her basket was brimming with fresh produce and the air was filled with the fading hustle and bustle of the market. Emma's thoughts swirled around the intriguing footman. There was something about him – his charm, his wit, his sophistication – that had stirred feelings she didn't quite understand.

Arriving home, she found Uncle Edward pacing by the front door, a scowl deeply etched on his face. "Where have you been, Emma? Luke has been asking about you." His voice was gruff, filled with repressed frustration.

"I'm sorry, Uncle Edward," Emma said, keeping her voice steady. "The market was busier than usual today."

"Excuses, always excuses," Edward sighed, his fingers pinching the bridge of his nose. "Dinner should've been ready an hour ago. Can't you do anything right?"

"I'll get right on it," Emma promised, ignoring the sharp sting of his words. She set her basket down and headed to the kitchen, feeling Edward's disapproving gaze on her back.

The harshness of Edward's voice and his constant disapproval was a stark contrast to the banter she had shared with William earlier. In her mind's eye, she saw William's friendly smile, heard his hearty laugh, and felt the warmth of his praise. Her heart longed for more of such kindness, so different from the harsh world she was used to.

As Emma began to prepare the evening meal, she couldn't help but imagine a different life. A life filled with laughter and companionship, where she wasn't just a pair of helping hands but a person of worth. She thought of William, and how he had made her feel seen, valued. She didn't know what the future held, but for the first time in a long time, she felt a spark of hope that there might be more for her out there.

As she chopped vegetables and stirred the stew, she found herself lost in dreams of a different life. However, she was well aware that dreams were a luxury she could ill afford. Squaring her shoulders, Emma focused on the task at hand, allowing the rhythm of cooking to ease her troubled mind. For now, she had a job to do and a family to care for. Tomorrow, however, was another day, and who knew what it might bring?

With a final glance out of the window, the setting sun painting the sky in hues of red and gold, Emma couldn't help but allow herself one final, wistful thought. "Perhaps," she murmured, "perhaps one day..."

Chapter Nine

William Maxwell

William Maxwell watched as Emma disappeared amongst the bustling market crowd, her simple dress swaying with each determined step she took. He felt a pang of guilt strike him, knowing he'd deceived her. The corner of his mouth tilted upwards in a self-deprecating smile. It was a strange twist, a rich man pretending to be a footman.

Shaking off the slight regret, William turned and walked down the cobblestone street to where his actual footman, Thomas, stood waiting beside a sleek black carriage. The pair of well-groomed horses snorted in the chilly air, their breath forming small clouds.

"Sir," Thomas bowed respectfully, opening the carriage door. "I trust your errand was successful?"

"In a manner of speaking," William said, stepping inside the plush interior of the carriage. He settled against the velvet seat, his gaze drifting back towards the market. "I met an interesting young woman."

"Oh?" Thomas raised an eyebrow as he climbed into the driver's seat. "Does this have anything to do with your... disguise?"

"I wanted to get a feel for the people, the real people of this town," William explained, a thoughtful look crossing his face. "You can't truly know a place from the comfort of a mansion and through the reports of servants, can you?"

Thomas didn't respond. He simply flicked the reins and the carriage lurched forward. Inside, William leaned back, letting his thoughts wander back to Emma. He was taken aback by her frankness, her tenacity, and her dedication to her family. And now that he knew her situation, he felt a strange urge to help her, to see her smile genuinely.

"Take the scenic route back to the manor, Thomas," he ordered, his gaze fixed on the passing town. He needed some time to figure out his next steps. The image of Emma's radiant smile and the sound of her lilting laughter was etched into his memory.

"Yes, sir," Thomas responded, guiding the horses onto a longer, quieter road. The rolling countryside sprawled before them, providing William with the perfect backdrop for his thoughts.

William's guilt bubbled up once again. He'd lied to Emma, pretended to be something he wasn't. He wasn't sure what he could do to make it right, but he was certain of one thing. He needed to see Emma again, this time, as the man he truly was.

Thomas guided the carriage through the iron gates and onto the expansive grounds of William's estate. The manor house loomed ahead, a grand structure made of age-worn stone and draped in ivy. It was the kind of place that was designed to impress, to assert the wealth and power of the owner. Yet, as grand as it was, it had a touch of loneliness clinging to it.

Servants hurried around, performing their respective duties. The gardeners attended to the manicured hedges and flower beds, while the housemaids polished the large windows until they gleamed. There was a strict system, an order to things, and everyone knew their place.

Yet, despite the air of authority that William exuded, he was not an unkind master. He believed in sternness, not cruelty, in treating his staff with respect and dignity.

"Master Maxwell," his housekeeper, Mrs Reed, greeted him as he descended from the carriage. She was a stern woman with a heart of gold, who ran his household with an iron fist clad in a velvet glove.

"Mrs Reed," he nodded in greeting. "See that Thomas gets a hot meal. It's been a long morning."

"Certainly, sir," she replied, her grey eyes flashing with approval.

Stepping inside the manor, William was met with the familiar sights and sounds of his home. The grand foyer, with its high ceiling and impressive chandelier, was bustling with activity as footmen scurried about, carrying out their duties. His steward, Mr Bennett, was busy scribbling notes on a parchment. Upon noticing his master's return, he hastily got to his feet.

"Master Maxwell," he said, "There's a letter from the Duke of Henshaw, and your horse breeder has sent word about a new foal."

"Thank you, Bennett," William said. He walked up the grand staircase, his mind whirling. The day had brought about a change, an unexpected meeting that stirred feelings he had long since buried. Feelings of companionship, of domestic tranquillity, of love. He had never desired for a loveless marriage based solely on social rank and property. His heart had always yearned for something more, for a bond rooted in shared interests and mutual affection.

As he retired to his private study, his mind wandered back to Emma. He could see her now, laughing and full of life, in the grand drawing-room of his manor. He could hear her voice filling the silence of his lonely home, making it lively and homey. The thought brought a smile to his lips.

William Maxwell, the wealthy, elusive bachelor, longed for a wife, a partner to share his life with. And perhaps, just perhaps, he had found her in a spirited, young woman from the market.

Chapter Ten

As Emma moved through the crowded market, she recognised the familiar figure of William. His dark hair and tall, lean figure stood out amongst the hustle and bustle of the market crowd. He was haggling over fresh loaves of bread with Mr Parker, the old baker.

"Mr Maxwell," she greeted him, a smile playing on her lips.

He turned around, his face breaking into a warm smile at the sight of her. "Miss Emma, a pleasure to see you again."

They fell into an easy conversation, discussing everything from their daily lives to their favourite foods. The market buzzed around them, but for Emma, the world seemed to narrow to just her and William.

"I must admit," William began, a twinkle in his eyes, "I never thought I'd enjoy the task of haggling for bread so much."

Emma laughed, "It's not just any bread. Mr Parker's loaves are famous around here."

There was a simplicity to their exchanges, a light-heartedness that Emma had rarely experienced in her life. In this moment, she wasn't just the girl who was burdened with household chores and childcare. She was a young woman enjoying a friendly chat with a charming gentleman.

"You have quite the taste for the finer things in life," William teased, holding up a fresh loaf. His light-hearted remark made her blush, but she met his teasing with a playful roll of her eyes.

As the day wore on, Emma found herself relaxing into the conversation, her initial wariness about William easing away. She felt a connection with him, something she hadn't experienced before. Her days were usually filled with chores and care for her cousins. She rarely had the chance to make friends, to have the kind of casual, engaging conversations she was having now with William.

Looking at William, she noticed the warm smile on his face, the way his eyes crinkled at the corners when he laughed. He seemed genuinely interested in her, in her life and her thoughts. This was a far cry from her interactions with Uncle Edward, who seemed to view her as little more than a maid.

Their banter continued as they strolled through the market, with William's attention seemingly riveted on Emma. She was drawn to his charm, his easy-going nature, and found herself asking more about his life.

"What about you, Mr Maxwell?" she asked, her curiosity piqued. "What's life like for a footman?"

His eyes flicked away momentarily before a half smile played on his lips. "It's... interesting, Emma. A footman's life involves a great deal of running around, of course. There is a certain rhythm to it that I find... satisfying."

His evasive answer, his hesitance, stirred a flicker of suspicion in Emma's mind. She pondered the possibility that there was more to William than he let on. Yet, she shrugged off the thought, not wanting it to spoil their pleasant exchange.

As they meandered through the market, Emma found herself daydreaming. What would it be like to be married to someone like William? A footman he might be, but there was an unmistakable air of refinement about him. He was kind, respectful, and had a way of making her feel special.

Caught up in her thoughts, she blurted out, "Mr Maxwell, do you think your master would be in need of a maid? I'm looking for work at the moment..."

William seemed taken aback, his eyes widened in surprise. "Oh," he stammered, a hint of panic in his eyes. "You are too kind-hearted to be just a maid. Besides, I fear my master wouldn't be in the market for more staff currently."

His hasty dismissal of her suggestion puzzled Emma. Yet, she took it in stride, a part of her relieved that she hadn't been too forward. Her growing attraction towards him remained her secret.

"Where…where is the estate you work at William?" Emma asked hesitantly, not sure if he would tell her.

There was a long pause. William had lied to her about being a footman, he didn't want to lie anymore, telling her the address, which Emma had not heard of before. "It's not too far from here, actually."

Emma was glad. That meant that she might run into him more often.

As they reached the town square, the fading sun cast long shadows around them. "Well, Miss Emma," William began, tipping his hat off in a cordial farewell, "it was a pleasure spending time with you."

She nodded, her cheeks flushed from the pleasant afternoon. "The pleasure was mine, Mr Maxwell."

With a final wave, they parted, each heading in different directions. Emma moved through the dimming streets, a lightness in her step. The afternoon spent in William's company had felt like a brief escape from her laborious existence. She turned the corner onto her street, the familiar sight of the family home coming into view.

As Emma stepped through the front door, a harsh voice cut through the quiet. "Where have you been?" Uncle Edward barked, his brow furrowed in an angry scowl.

Startled, she turned to him. "I was out at the market, getting..."

"I'm not a fool, Emma," Edward interrupted, his voice low and dangerous. "The market doesn't take all afternoon. You've been seen."

Seen? The word made her stomach drop. "I don't understand..."

"With that man," Edward spat, "Meeting with him, laughing with him, walking around town as if you're some lady of leisure."

"I... it wasn't like that," Emma stammered, a lump forming in her throat. "We just ran into each other. He's just a friend..."

"I won't hear it," Edward interjected, cutting her off. "You've responsibilities here, and I won't tolerate such behaviour."

"But Uncle..."

"I said I won't hear it!" he roared, his face turning a deep shade of red. Emma flinched at his anger, her own feelings of happiness from the afternoon evaporating.

Edward didn't storm off, instead, he stood tall in the entryway, his jaw tight with anger. "You're a bad influence on my children," he snarled, his voice resounding in the tight space. "Just when they were getting used to you, you bring in this nonsense."

"I... I didn't mean to..." Emma stuttered, but Edward cut her off.

"And what about Flora?" he continued, heedless of her interruption. "She's barely fifteen, and now she'll have her head filled with ideas about men and marriage. It's not right!"

"Uncle Edward, I assure you, I've never discussed anything inappropriate with her..."

His lips curled into a bitter smile. "Oh, I believe you, Emma. You don't need to say a word. You just need to flutter your eyelashes at some man and she'll think it's a woman's place to chase after them."

The harsh accusation left her reeling. Edward wasn't finished, though. "You're just like my wife," he spat out, his face twisted with anger.

Emma felt a sharp pang at the mention of his wife - her Aunt, who had left Edward years ago. "Uncle, I would never..."

"She left us for some rich man, thinking he'd give her a better life," he growled, his gaze hard on her. "He never cared about her, not like I did. Is that what you want, Emma? To chase after men for money and end up alone?"

The question was like a slap in the face. Emma felt her cheeks burn with humiliation and anger. "No," she replied quietly, her voice shaking, "I don't want that. I just... I just want a friend."

"Well, then you're better off without friends like him," Edward declared. He pointed a stern finger at her. "You've responsibilities here. Your focus should be on this family and not some man you met at the market."

"Uncle Edward, please listen to me-"

"Enough of your protests, Emma!" Edward's shout resonated in the small space, a wave of heat and anger that seemed to fill the room.

"Uncle Edward, I haven't done anything wrong," she tried again, her voice small in the face of his fury.

The man before her was no longer the familiar, sullen figure she had lived with for the last six years. Now, he was a pillar of wrath, his ire focused squarely on her.

"If you're going to behave like a spoiled, ungrateful brat, then you can leave!" he roared, his words like a whip, cutting deep and drawing blood. Emma recoiled, feeling as though she had been physically slapped.

Edward was breathing hard, his face a dark mask of fury. "Flora is old enough to handle the household duties now," he continued in a tight voice, his gaze unwavering. "She doesn't need your...your bad influence."

"Uncle Edward, please..." Emma started to say, her voice choking on her own tears.

"No, Emma!" he interrupted. "Pack your things. You will leave this house by Friday."

His words rang in her ears like a death knell. The finality of his command was stark and uncompromising. He left her there in the entryway, his echoing footsteps a bitter farewell.

Emma stood in the silence of the now empty room, her heart pounding. Her hands shook as she absorbed the magnitude of his words. She had no home, no family. Uncle Edward was all she had left, and now he was casting her aside.

A sob escaped her lips, but she quickly choked it back. No, she wouldn't let Edward see her cry. She wouldn't give him the satisfaction. She had three days. Three days to pack her belongings, three days to find a new place, three days to say goodbye to the only family she'd ever known.

***

Emma found herself buried under the covers of her small bed, eyes scrunched shut against the pain. Her suitcase lay at the foot of the bed, still empty. It wasn't as if she had much to pack.

It was a quiet knock that finally broke Emma from her tearful stupor. She quickly wiped her eyes and unlocked the door to find Flora and Beatrice standing in the hallway, their faces etched with concern and sadness. Beatrice, in particular, seemed to be on the verge of tears herself.

"We heard...," Beatrice began, her voice trembled slightly. She glanced at Flora who squeezed her hand, urging her to continue. "Father wouldn't listen to me, Emma. He said you're leaving, that he won't change his mind."

Emma swallowed hard, blinking away the fresh tears that threatened to spill from her eyes. "I'm sorry, Beatrice," she whispered, her voice barely audible. "I didn't mean for this to happen."

Beatrice gave her a tremulous smile, rushing forward to wrap Emma in a tight hug. "I'm sorry, Emma," she whispered fiercely into her hair. "You didn't do anything wrong."

Flora nodded, her usually stoic face softened with affection. "You're our sister,

Emma, and we love you. Father... he's just... he's never been the same since mother left."

A sad silence descended on the room. The three girls huddled together, their shared grief uniting them in this moment of sorrow.

"I don't want to leave," Emma finally confessed, her voice muffled against Beatrice's shoulder. "But I don't think I have a choice."

Flora squeezed her hand, her gaze steady and resolute. "We don't want you to go."

The room was hushed, the only sound was the soft sniffling of the sisters. It was a moment that was almost sacred in its intimacy, as if the weight of their shared sorrow had created a silent sanctuary.

A soft creak from the door interrupted their vigil. They all turned to see Luke standing hesitantly in the doorway, his young face marred with concern. Without a word, he padded towards the bed and climbed onto it, snuggling next to Emma.

"I don't want you to go, Emma," Luke confessed, his voice shaky. He reached up to tenderly kiss her forehead, his small hands clutching at her sleeve. "I tried to tell Father, but he wouldn't listen... he shouted at me."

Emma wrapped her arms around Luke, pulling him closer. She felt a lump in her throat as she took in the brave face of her ten-year-old cousin. Despite his tender age, he had grown to be a compassionate and kind-hearted boy.

"Oh, Luke," she whispered, her voice choked with emotion. She kissed his forehead, trying to offer comfort. "I don't want to leave either. I wish... I wish things could be different."

Luke nodded, snuggling deeper into her arms. His sincerity, his innocent affection, only made Emma's heart ache more.

"Emma," Flora interjected, her voice steady. She reached out to gently brush a stray lock of hair from Emma's face. "We're all going to miss you so much; but we also know you're strong, and you'll find your way."

Emma glanced at Flora, the quiet resolve in her eyes was a stark contrast to the sadness in her voice. The certainty in Flora's words offered an unexpected comfort. She wasn't alone, her family was with her, despite the circumstances.

Beatrice, who had been silent for a while, finally spoke up. "Papa doesn't know what he's doing. He's lost, Emma, but that doesn't mean you have to be."

Emma could only nod, her throat too tight for words. She pulled Beatrice, Flora, and Luke into an embrace, clinging to the warmth of their shared love.

"I don't know what will happen," Emma admitted, her voice barely more than a whisper. "I promise you, I won't forget you. I won't forget our time together."

In the quiet of their shared room, amidst the turmoil of their shattered family, the four of them made a promise to each other. No matter where they ended up, no matter the distance that separated them, they would remain a family. In spirit, if not in name. Their bond, stronger than any storm, would endure.

"Listen," Emma began, her voice wavering but steady. "I promise I'll keep in touch. I'll write to you, and we can meet when possible. This isn't goodbye, not really. It's just... just a promise to see you later."

The words hung in the air, echoing in the silent room. There was a certain melancholy to them, a reluctant acceptance of the reality they were facing. The room was heavy with the silent promise, the unspoken understanding that they were not parting ways forever.

"We will hold you to that, Emma," Flora said, her voice firm. She was the oldest of the siblings, and the weight of her role was evident in her serious demeanour.

Emma nodded, offering them a small smile. She had always admired Flora's resilience and strength. Even in this difficult situation, her cousin stood strong, unyielding. She was a rock amidst the storm, a beacon of hope.

Slowly, they started packing Emma's belongings. The process was sombre, each folded garment, each tucked away trinket, a reminder of the years they had shared. They worked in silence, their movements punctuated by the occasional sniffle or suppressed sob.

Emma felt a lump in her throat as she folded her clothes, her fingers tracing the familiar patterns and fabrics. Each piece was a memory, a moment captured in time. The blue dress she wore for their family picnic last summer, the apron she had received on her last birthday. Each held a piece of her past, her time spent with the family she loved.

As they neared the end of their task, Beatrice suddenly let out a soft whimper. She was clutching one of Emma's sweaters, her tears soaking the soft fabric. Emma moved to her side, wrapping an arm around her as Beatrice sobbed into the sweater.

"Promise you'll be okay, Emma," Beatrice choked out, her words muffled by the fabric.

"I promise, Bea," Emma whispered, her own tears welling up. "I'll be okay."

With that, they finished packing, the room once filled with their shared laughter and stories now felt barren, the packed suitcase a stark reminder of their impending parting. As they looked at each other, the love and the bond they shared was palpable, a silver thread binding them together.

With the room bathed in the soft light of the dying day, their world felt on the brink of a significant shift, a moment in time that they would remember with a bittersweet ache.

The room was silent, their goodbyes still unspoken. In their hearts, they knew this was only a temporary farewell, a pause in their shared story. Yet as Emma gazed around the room one last time, her heart ached with a profound sadness. The door closed behind her, the click echoing in the silent room like a poignant end to a cherished chapter.

Chapter Eleven

The day had been a whirlwind of chores and secret, teary glances exchanged with Flora and Beatrice. The house felt colder, the silence louder. Emma spent most of her day avoiding Edward, focusing on the mundane tasks that kept her busy. Her heart felt heavy, the reality of her departure settling in like an unwelcome guest.

As the evening drew near, the house grew quieter. Flora and Beatrice were out, visiting a friend. Luke had been sent to the neighbours. Edward was in his study, leaving Emma to face her departure alone.

When the time came, she took one last look at her room. The sight of the empty bed and barren walls left a sour taste in her mouth. A sense of finality washed over her. She swallowed hard, picked up her suitcase, and made her way downstairs.

Edward was standing in the hallway as she descended the stairs, a stiff, imposing figure. His face was a mask of impassivity, but his eyes were hard. Emma tried to steady her voice, pushing away the lump in her throat.

"Uncle Edward," she started, "I...I'm leaving."

The silence that followed was deafening. She could hear the faint ticking of the clock in the hallway, each second stretching into an eternity. Edward finally looked at her, his gaze cold and distant.

"Good," he muttered, his voice harsh. "It's about time."

The words stung, a bitter reminder of the chasm that had grown between them. Emma wanted to defend herself, to make him understand, but she knew it was futile. Instead, she nodded, turning away to hide the tears welling up in her eyes.

With her heart heavy and the snow falling outside, Emma stepped out of the house she had called home. The cold air bit into her skin, the falling snowflakes a stark contrast against the dark night. She trudged through the thick layer of snow, her steps leaving a trail behind her.

The warmth of the house disappeared behind her, replaced by the biting cold of the winter evening. She pulled her cloak tighter around her, her breath forming clouds in the frosty air. Emma glanced back one last time, the house now a mere silhouette against the snowy landscape. A chapter of her life had ended, and another was about to begin.

As the frigid wind blew stronger, Emma's steps began to falter. The snowflakes dancing in the air seemed less magical now, biting into her exposed skin like tiny shards of ice. Every breath was a struggle, her lungs filled with the icy air. She trudged through the thick snow, her heart heavy, her mind a whirl of thoughts.

Eventually, she reached a boarding house. The light escaping from the windows seemed like a beacon in the otherwise desolate street, and Emma felt a tiny flicker of hope. She knocked, a soft, hesitant rap against the worn-out wooden door.

A stern-faced woman answered, her eyes examining Emma suspiciously. "What do you want?" she asked, her tone harsh and unwelcoming.

"I...I need a room," Emma said, her voice shaky from the cold. She reached into her pocket, pulling out the small amount of money Flora and Beatrice had managed to save for her.

The woman's eyes narrowed, taking in the pitiful amount. "This won't even cover a day," she sneered. Emma felt a pang of embarrassment, her cheeks flushing in the cold.

"I...I can work," she stammered, desperate. "Cooking, cleaning...anything you need."

The woman laughed, a harsh, grating sound that sent a chill down Emma's spine. "Don't need another maid," she said, her eyes glinting cruelly. "We've plenty. And we don't give charity here."

"But I-"

The woman didn't let her finish. With a cruel twist of her mouth, she slammed the door shut. Emma stood there, stunned, as the reality of her situation sunk in. She was alone, penniless, and without a place to stay. The world seemed to grow colder around her, the snow swirling in an unending dance of mockery.

For a moment, she stood there, the harsh wind cutting through her cloak. Her body shivered violently from the cold, her fingers numb. She wanted to knock again, plead for the woman's mercy, but her pride held her back. She had suffered enough humiliation for one day.

With a sigh, she trudged back into the cold, the harsh wind blowing against her. The snowflakes swirled around her, as if in a cruel celebration of her predicament. She didn't know where she was going, didn't have a plan. All she knew was that she couldn't stand there anymore.

Emma's next attempt was a small, rundown boarding house tucked away in a less frequented part of the town. The man at the door, a grizzled older fellow with a distinct limp, eyed her money with disdain.

"This won't even cover the meals," he grunted, handing the coins back to her. "Can't be giving rooms away for free."

"I can work," Emma said, echoing the same words she'd said at the previous place. "I can clean, cook...anything."

The man's eyes, previously apathetic, hardened. "I've got plenty to do those things already. Ain't need another mouth to feed."

With that, the door shut, leaving Emma alone once again in the biting cold. She stood there, her heart aching with the repeated rejections. Was there truly no place for her?

The last place Emma tried was a modest inn on the outskirts of the town. The innkeeper, a kindly looking woman with a matronly figure, listened to her story with sympathy. When Emma showed her the pitiful amount of money, the innkeeper sighed.

"I'm sorry, dear," she said gently, "but we run a business here. We can't afford to take people in without proper payment."

"I can work for my stay," Emma pleaded, her desperation apparent.

The innkeeper shook her head. "We have enough help already. I'm sorry, my girl, I truly am."

Emma thanked her for her time and left, the last bit of her hope extinguishing with the closing of the door. Her legs felt heavy, her body weary. Her eyes stung with unshed tears, her heart aching with despair.

She thought about going back to Edward's. Maybe he would take pity on her, let her stay until she could find a job. She quickly pushed the thought away. He had made it clear - he didn't want her there.

As the last light of the day faded, Emma found herself wandering the town aimlessly. The snowfall grew heavier, the wind more vicious. Her fingers and toes were numb, her breaths coming out in shaky gasps. She feared that if she didn't find shelter soon, she might not survive the night.

She passed by darkened houses and closed shops, their windows casting long shadows on the snow-covered streets. There was no one to ask for help, no one to share her plight. She was utterly alone, lost amidst the swirling snow and her own mounting fear.

Her thoughts turned to Owen and Abigail, to the warmth and love she had once known. She wished with all her heart that she could go back, rewind to the times when she was surrounded by laughter and joy. Those days were long gone, and Emma was alone in the cold, left to fend for herself.

In the pit of her desperation, a spark of hope ignited. William. He had mentioned where he worked. Perhaps, just perhaps, his master might have need of a housemaid or be inclined to charity. Emma knew it was a long shot, a slim hope clinging to a thread, but it was all she had.

She began the long, frigid walk towards the address. The cold pierced through her thin cloak and the wind whipped her hair about her face, but she pressed on. She followed the winding roads of the town until they gave way to cobbled streets lined with tall, grand houses. The snowflakes danced under the soft glow of the streetlamps, painting an eerily beautiful picture that did little to ease her mounting anxiety.

Finally, she arrived at the address William had mentioned. The house, or rather, the manor, took her breath away. It was enormous, grander than anything she had ever seen. Its majestic facade was adorned with intricate carvings, the windows large and glowing with inviting warmth. The grounds were immaculately kept, even under the layer of snow. It was like something out of a fairy tale, and Emma felt distinctly out of place.

With a deep breath, she approached the door, the grandeur of the place making her feel smaller than ever. Her knock echoed through the quiet of the night, and it wasn't long before the door opened.

The doorman was an elderly man, his expression stern, yet his eyes held a certain kindness. He looked at her, standing there, shivering and miserable, and his stern expression softened a bit.

"Can I help you, Miss?" he asked, his tone brusque, but not unkind.

"I...I'm looking for William Maxwell, I believe he works as a footman here," Emma managed to stutter out, the cold making her words come out in shaky whispers. She explained her situation, the desperation evident in her voice.

The doorman studied her for a long moment, his gaze thoughtful. The silence seemed to stretch on forever before he finally responded.

"What makes you think…. Ah. I'll see what I can do, Miss," he said, his voice holding a hint of sympathy. "Wait here."

The door closed with a soft click, leaving Emma alone again on the grand entrance, the wind and snow her only company. Her teeth chattered uncontrollably as she clutched her thin cloak around her, staring at the impressive door, praying for some salvation.

After what felt like an eternity, the door opened again, the warm light from inside casting a glow over the doorman. His expression was inscrutable, a blend of amusement and sympathy.

"He is sleeping," he informed her. "It's quite late, you see."

Emma nodded, her heart sinking. The cold was beginning to seep into her bones now, a gnawing pain that seemed to mirror the ache in her heart.

"But..." the doorman continued, the glint in his eyes growing, "I think you have misunderstood something here."

Emma frowned, uncertain. She was on the verge of asking why he was amused when he chuckled, shaking his head slightly.

"Poor girl," he said, more to himself than her. "What made you think Master Maxwell was a footman?"

Emma blinked at him, her confusion giving way to shock. "He...he said..." she stammered, her mind reeling from the revelation.

The doorman chuckled again. "William is a strange man," he admitted. "He always liked to play the servant rather than the master. Make no mistake, he is the master of this house."

Instead of the expected warmth and reassurance, the doorman's friendly gaze hardened into a mocking smirk. He laughed, a deep rumbling sound that echoed ominously off the high walls.

"You thought our master was a footman? Here I was thinking you were another desperate woman trying to ensnare the Master's wealth. You thought him a footman. "

With that, he barked another round of laughter, his body shaking with mirth. Emma felt her cheeks burn, a mix of shame and anger welling up inside her. Her heart pounded against her chest as she processed his cruel words. The cold that had seeped into her bones now felt like a harsh sting.

"How dare you laugh at me!" Emma snapped, her voice shaking. She felt a fresh wave of tears prickling at her eyes. The doorman simply shrugged, clearly unbothered by her anger.

"Should I have lied to you instead, Miss?" He retorted. "You're the one who mixed up a Master for a footman. You made your own mess. Can't blame a man for enjoying a good laugh."

The tears that had welled up in Emma's eyes now flowed freely down her cheeks. It wasn't just the biting cold or the doorman's callousness that hurt; it was the sense of betrayal. William had lied to her, played with her feelings. For what, a laugh? Was she just another joke to him?

"No one asked for your judgment," Emma shot back, wiping her eyes with the back of her hand. She was cold, humiliated, and, most of all, hurt. "I don't need your pity or your mockery. Good evening."

With that, she turned on her heel, intending to leave. She didn't know where she would go, but anywhere was better than being the butt of the joke for the wealthy residents of this grand manor.

As she descended the steps, her mind echoed with the doorman's cruel laughter, the hurt in her heart a stark contrast to the beautiful house that stood tall behind her. She clutched her cloak tighter around herself, the feeling of betrayal a painful lump in her chest as she navigated the cold and dark grounds of the manor, of a world that had once again turned its back on her.

The icy wind felt like sharp needles on her skin as Emma stumbled down the cobbled walkway, away from the grand manor. Her heart was in turmoil, torn between humiliation, anger, and the deepest sense of betrayal. The cold had permeated through her threadbare coat, but it was the frosty pain in her heart that felt unbearable.

Every moment she'd spent with William replayed in her mind. His charming smiles, his easy banter, his friendly demeanour - they all seemed like a cruel joke now. A cold, harsh joke at her expense. His deception was a fresh wound on her already battered spirit, and the pain was raw, searing.

"I'm such a fool," she murmured to herself, her voice barely above a whisper. Emma was so consumed by her thoughts that she didn't realise she had stopped moving. She was standing still, just outside the iron gate of the manor, the majestic house a dark silhouette against the moonlit sky. She clutched the cold bars of the gate, her heart pounding against her ribs.

Emma stared blankly at the beautifully carved gate, her mind reeling. She felt like a small, insignificant creature against the vast expanse of wealth and power that lay beyond. She had dared to hope for a better life, had let herself dream of a future where she could be happy. Now, those dreams lay shattered at her feet, crushed under the weight of harsh reality.

"Emma, what did you expect? That he'd sweep you off your feet? That he'd save you from your pitiful life?" She muttered to herself, her voice filled with self-loathing. Her vision blurred as hot tears welled up in her eyes, spilling down her cheeks and freezing in the cold night air.

"Maybe...maybe he didn't mean to hurt me," she thought desperately, trying to salvage some hope from the wreckage of her dreams. The doorman's mocking laughter echoed in her mind, and she shook her head, berating herself for her foolishness.

The bitter cold seemed to seep into her very soul as she stood there, trying to muster the courage to walk away. Emma's heart felt like a heavy stone in her chest, and the cold seemed to reflect her inner turmoil. She was lost, with no place to call home, no shoulder to lean on. All she had were her shattered dreams and a heart full of regret.

Chapter Twelve

The echo of unfamiliar voices drifting upstairs roused William from his sleep. Pushing off the plush quilt, he rose from the bed, the quiet murmurs intriguing him enough to investigate. As he descended the grand staircase, he found his doorman and butler engaged in a hushed conversation.

"James, what's the matter?" William asked, glancing at the front door which still swung gently open, letting in a flurry of snowflakes.

"Sir...a young woman came to the door. She was a blonde, quite pretty, but she seemed to be under the impression you were a footman. I saw her off, sir," James explained, offering a faint smile that held a hint of derision.

The description hit William like a punch to the gut. He could picture only one woman. "Emma?" he breathed out, the image of her golden hair and bright blue eyes filling his mind.

"I never asked for her name, Master Maxwell," James answered, seeming taken aback by William's sudden serious tone.

Without another word, William brushed past him, pulling on his coat as he stormed out into the biting cold. His heart pounded as he raced towards the manor gates, his breath coming out in icy puffs.

As he rounded the corner, he spotted a small figure in the distance. The golden hair, the slender form – it was unmistakably Emma. He ran towards her, calling out her name into the silent night.

"Emma! Wait!" He caught up with her just at the gates, his chest heaving from the exertion and the cold.

She spun around, her eyes wide with surprise, then narrowing into a glare. "You?!" she spat, her voice a venomous whisper that stung more than the cold. "You lied to me!"

"Emma, I..." he started, reaching out to her. She took a step back, her expression hardening.

"You had your fun, didn't you?" she accused, her voice trembling with anger and hurt. "Making a fool of me, pretending to be someone you're not!"

"Emma, please. I never intended... Let's go inside, we can talk about this," he implored, his eyes pleading with hers.

"Inside? Your grand mansion?" she sneered, her eyes welling up with angry tears. "I'd rather freeze to death."

"Emma," he pleaded again, rushing to her side as she started to walk away. "At least tell me what happened."

"Uncle Edward had me leave," she spat bitterly, hugging herself against the freezing cold. "Apparently, I'm too much of a bad influence to be around."

Her words stung, but he forced himself to keep calm. "Come inside, Emma. It's freezing out here."

"I'm not taking your charity, William," she shot back, her eyes aflame with stubbornness and defiance.

"I'm not offering charity," he countered. "I have a job for you."

That seemed to surprise her, her heated glare softening a touch. "What sort of job? I would make a good maid, goodness knows I've been acting as Uncle Edward's for long enough."

"No, not a maid," he shook his head. "I have a sister, Ruth. She's been ailing for some time now, and she needs someone to keep her company, look after her. I...I think you'd be perfect for the job."

Emma blinked at him, her anger slowly being replaced with confusion and then a cautious hope. "You want me to be a...a companion?"

"Yes," he nodded earnestly, taking a step closer. "A friend. It's honest work, Emma, and I think Ruth would like you."

For a moment, she was silent, staring at him through the falling snowflakes. Then, slowly, she gave a small nod. "All right," she said, her voice barely audible above the wind. "I'll do it."

A wave of relief washed over William. He offered her a small, thankful smile, before leading her back towards the grand manor that would now become her new home. As they walked, the snowflakes seemed less harsh, the night less cold.

As they trekked back through the winding pathways that led to the manor, William broke the silence. "Emma, I need to apologise. I never intended to hurt you," he confessed, his voice barely above a whisper.

She turned to face him, her blue eyes piercing through the falling snow. "You lied to me, William," she accused, her voice cold. "You made me believe that you were someone you're not."

"I know," he admitted, his gaze falling to the snow-covered ground. "I wanted you to like me for who I am, not for my wealth or status. I see now how unfair it was to deceive you. I promise, Emma, I won't lie to you again."

She remained silent for a moment, studying him. "Do you really mean that, William?" she asked, her voice softened.

He looked back at her, his heart pounding in his chest. "I do, Emma," he assured. "I want to earn your trust again. I...I would like for us to make up in time for Christmas."

She gave him a long, searching look before she finally nodded. "All right, William. I'll give you a chance. It's going to take time," she warned. "You have to prove to me that you're someone I can trust."

"I will, Emma," he vowed. "I'll do whatever it takes."

They continued their walk back to the manor in silence, the tension between them slowly melting away like the snow under their feet. They had a long journey ahead, filled with rebuilding trust and mending fences. For now, they had a starting point, and that was enough.

As they entered the grand foyer of the manor, the warmth of the house washed over them, dispelling the biting cold that clung to their clothes. James, the doorman who had mocked her, stood by the fireplace, his face paling as they walked in.

With a stern expression, William addressed the doorman. "James, we will discuss your actions later in the morning. You will be dealt with fairly, but know that your actions tonight were unacceptable."

James looked suitably chastised, but it was the silent look Emma shot him that really hit home. There was no smug satisfaction on her face, no triumph in her gaze. Instead, she bore the look of someone who had been wronged, but was willing to move past it.

Turning his attention to Emma, William guided her through the mansion's ornate corridors to a guest room. "I hope this room will be comfortable for you," he said. "I'll ask the cook to prepare something warm for you to eat."

Emma gave a small nod, her lips curving into a ghost of a smile. She was tired and hurt, but she had a roof over her head and a future that wasn't as bleak as it seemed a few hours ago.

As William left her to settle in, he couldn't help but feel a sense of hope. There were wounds to be healed and trust to be regained, but he was certain that they were on the path to reconciliation. Tomorrow, he promised himself, would be a new day, a new beginning. A start to a hopeful journey.

Chapter Thirteen

The morning found Emma in the rose-walled chamber that Ruth called her own. It was a room full of life, filled with books, flowers, and art. The frail girl lay in an ornate bed, propped up by many pillows, her pale skin contrasted sharply against the dark satin of the covers. Her gaze was clear and bright, though, a testament to the vitality that remained within her.

"Hello," Ruth said, a shy smile gracing her face as Emma stepped inside. "You must be Emma. William has told me all about you."

"Has he now?" Emma said, a note of amusement in her voice as she took a seat by Ruth's side.

Ruth's eyes twinkled. "Don't worry, all good things, I assure you." She studied Emma with an openness that put her at ease. "He said you'd be my new companion. I hope that's all right."

Emma couldn't help but return the younger girl's smile. "Of course, it's all right, Ruth. I'm grateful for the opportunity."

The gratitude in Ruth's gaze was genuine. "I should be the one thanking you, Emma. It's been so lonely here, and I'm glad for the company. You're so...alive."

Their conversation flowed naturally from there, as they found shared interests in literature and art. Ruth was well-educated, thoughtful and witty. They laughed together at Ruth's dry sense of humour, and Emma listened as the younger girl shared her hopes for a life outside the confines of her illness.

When William joined them later, he looked on at the scene with evident relief. His gaze met Emma's, and for the first time since she'd known him, she saw the burden of worry easing off his shoulders. He thanked her, his voice earnest, his smile genuine.

There was no doubt in Emma's mind then that she'd found a place where she could belong, a family she could call her own. A sense of peace washed over her as she returned William's smile, realising that despite the upheavals in her life, she might have found something beautiful amidst the chaos.

Leaving Ruth's room, Emma made her way to her own new quarters, which were much more lavish than anything she'd ever been accustomed to. The high ceiling, the plush carpet underfoot, the delicate lace curtains dancing in the gentle morning breeze - it was all so overwhelming, yet alluring.

Before she could enter her room, a voice called her name, and she turned to see William leaning against a nearby wall. He was watching her, a gentle smile playing on his lips.

"You've made Ruth very happy, Emma. I cannot tell you how much it means to me to see her smile like that again," he confessed. His eyes were soft, mirroring the warmth in his voice.

"And it's not just Ruth," he continued. "Seeing you happy... it brings me joy as well.

I didn't realise how much I missed your smile until I saw it again."

Emma felt a flush creep up her cheeks. His words tugged at something inside her, something that yearned to believe him, to let him in. She wasn't sure if she was ready to forgive him yet, but she had to admit, the harsh edges of her anger were slowly smoothing out.

Seeing her blush, William's smile grew wider. He stepped forward, reaching out to place a gentle hand on her arm. "I meant what I said, Emma. I regret how I misled you and I want to make amends. I... I've missed you."

His honesty disarmed her. Emma looked at him, taking in the sincerity in his eyes, the yearning in his voice. The old attraction, the friendly banter, the moments of shared laughter - all those feelings started to resurface. Was it possible that she was falling for him? Her heart pounded at the thought.

"William," she said softly, her eyes meeting his. She hesitated, her mind a whirl of emotions, but she managed to get the words out. "I... I've missed you too. I'm still upset about what happened, but... I can't deny that there's something between us."

William's smile widened and there was relief in his eyes. He squeezed her arm gently before letting go. "Thank you, Emma. We'll take it one day at a time."

As she finally entered her new room, closing the door behind her, Emma allowed herself a small smile. One day at a time, she echoed in her thoughts. It felt like a promise. A promise of new beginnings, of healing and forgiveness... and perhaps, just perhaps, of love.

Chapter Fourteen

Ruth and Emma sat in the living room, with the large Christmas tree casting warm shadows on their faces. Tucked under a heavy blanket, Ruth was sitting by the roaring fireplace, her illness making her too weak to move much, but her spirit was as lively as ever. Her eyes sparkled with excitement as she watched Emma moving around the room, placing decorations around the room.

William sat on the other side, carefully sorting through an assortment of glass baubles and ornaments. The flicker of the fire danced in his eyes, giving them a warm, inviting glow.

"You're good at this, Emma," Ruth complimented as she watched Emma delicately hang a snowflake ornament on a branch of the tree. "You have a keen eye for beauty."

Emma smiled, but it was a melancholy one. "Christmas has always been a bit of a... difficult time for me," she confessed, her gaze dropping to the ground.

Ruth's expression softened and she looked over at her brother, who was listening intently. "Why is that?" she asked gently.

A moment of silence passed before Emma began to speak, her voice barely above a whisper. "My parents passed during the Christmas season. I was only twelve... and before that, I lived at an orphanage. Christmas there was almost non-existent."

William put down the ornament he was holding and looked at her, his eyes filled with sympathy. "Emma," he began, his voice quiet yet steady. "I'm truly sorry. I cannot even begin to imagine the pain you must've experienced."

Ruth reached out and placed a frail hand on Emma's. "I'm sorry, too - but now you have us. We'll make sure this Christmas is a good one."

Emma looked up, her eyes meeting Ruth's. They were filled with kindness and understanding. She glanced at William, who was watching her, his gaze steady and sincere. She nodded, her voice shaky but filled with gratitude. "Thank you, Ruth. Thank you, William. This is... the first time in a long time that I feel welcomed."

As they sat there, the room bathed in the warm light of the fireplace and the twinkling glow of the Christmas tree, Emma felt a strange feeling stir in her heart. It was a feeling she hadn't experienced in a long time - a sense of belonging, of being wanted and cared for. For the first time in a long time, she felt that maybe, just maybe, Christmas wouldn't be so difficult after all.

Under Ruth's watchful eyes, Emma and William continued their task of decorating the tree. Their work was accompanied by a soft hum of carols playing on an old gramophone, the cheerful notes of 'Deck the Halls' filling the warm living room.

Ruth sat comfortably by the fire, her pale skin illuminated by the gentle flames. She would hold out a hand, beckoning to

Emma or William, who would come to her side to collect the next ornament.

As the evening wore on, a rhythm established itself; Ruth would hand an ornament to William, who would pass it to Emma to be placed on the tree. They were working in harmony, their actions synchronised in a silent dance of Christmas spirit.

At one point, Emma reached up to hang a delicate glass star, but her hand wavered, and she stumbled. William was beside her in an instant, his hand gripping her elbow to steady her. Their bodies were close, his warmth seeping through her clothes, his scent – a mix of pine and winter air – enveloping her.

She looked up into his eyes, surprised to find him looking intently at her. The green in his eyes sparkled in the soft, festive light, mirroring the Christmas tree lights. His gaze held hers, a silent question lingering in the air.

Emma's heart pounded in her chest, her breath hitched as she realised that she had forgiven him. Despite his initial deception, he had proven himself to be genuine and kind. An urge to lean in, to close the distance between them and press her lips against his, welled up within her. But she forced the feeling back down, reminding herself of the impropriety of her thoughts.

Breaking their locked gaze, she pulled away from him and gave him a small smile. "Thank you, William," she murmured.

He nodded, his gaze lingering on her for a moment longer before he turned back to Ruth, who was watching the exchange with a knowing smile on her face.

The rest of the evening passed in pleasant camaraderie, the trio lost in the spirit of Christmas. As they finally stood back to admire their handiwork, the beautifully decorated tree casting a magical glow in the room, Emma felt a warmth in her chest. It was happiness, it was contentment, but above all, it was the stirrings of a love that was just beginning to bloom.

As the evening turned into night, the tantalising aroma of roast goose filled the manor, permeating each room with a scent that felt as much a part of Christmas as the decorations themselves. The warmth from the fire spread through the living room, its comforting heat enveloping them like a soft, welcoming blanket.

Emma, William, and Ruth took a break, settling down around the coffee table for a late evening tea. A teapot sat in the middle, tendrils of steam curling upwards from the spout. Warm scones, clotted cream and strawberry jam lay in a serving tray, tempting them with the promise of a hearty treat.

"Everything looks perfect," Ruth sighed contentedly, her eyes reflecting the twinkling Christmas tree lights.

William, who had been pouring the tea, looked up at his sister's words, his gaze following hers to the decorated tree. A soft smile graced his lips, his eyes holding a glint of happiness Emma hadn't seen before. "It does, doesn't it? Thanks to both of you."

Emma found herself returning his smile, her heart fluttering in her chest. "It was really enjoyable, I... I haven't had a Christmas like this before."

They continued their tea, the room filled with laughter, the clinking of cups, and the occasional popping of the firewood. There was a comforting rhythm in their banter, a sense of familiarity that made Emma feel at home.

Yet, beneath the warmth and happiness, there was an underlying current of apprehension. It was a feeling Emma knew all too well. It was the unease that came when she allowed herself to be too happy, too content. She couldn't shake off the feeling that this peace, this warmth would not last. Because every time she had felt this way, something bad had happened.

Chapter Fifteen

Emma sat on a chair next to Ruth's bed, their lunch of chicken soup and warm bread spread out on the small bedside table. Ruth was getting stronger, the rosy blush in her cheeks a stark contrast to the pale, fragile girl she had met just weeks before.

"Ruth," Emma began, sipping her soup. "If you don't mind my asking, what was the matter with you?"

Ruth looked at Emma, her pale blue eyes shining with a mixture of trepidation and relief. "I had pneumonia as a child, and sometimes in the winter my lungs get weak. It's not life-threatening but... I've been bedridden for quite some time," she explained.

Emma nodded, understanding. "I'm sorry to hear that, Ruth."

Ruth gave her a small smile. "It's all right, Emma. I'm getting better now, and that's what matters."

There was truth in Ruth's words. The sickly pallor was gone, replaced by a healthier glow. She ate her meals with vigour, a far cry from the weak girl who would only pick at her food. Each day, Emma could see the strength returning to Ruth.

Yet, a small part of Emma was filled with dread. Ruth's recovery was a good thing, an incredible blessing. Unfortunately, it also meant that Emma's role as Ruth's companion and caretaker would no longer be necessary. If Ruth were to completely recover, what place would Emma have in this manor? What place would she have in William's life?

These were questions she dared not voice out loud, but they echoed in her mind, a nagging fear that kept her up at night. For now, all Emma could do was enjoy the fleeting moments of happiness and pray that her fears were unfounded.

Emma forced a smile, pushing her worries to the back of her mind. She focused on Ruth, tucking her gently into her warm blanket as she continued to sip her soup.

"Emma, are you okay?" Ruth asked, her sharp eyes scrutinizing Emma's face.

"Of course, Ruth," Emma replied quickly, trying to mask the uncertainty in her eyes.

Ruth squinted at her, her gaze piercing. "You're not a very good liar, Emma. Something's troubling you."

Emma sighed, taking Ruth's delicate hand into hers. "I promise you, Ruth, everything's fine. Let's just focus on your recovery, okay?"

Ruth nodded, still looking a little unsure. Then she broke into a warm smile, squeezing Emma's hand. "You know, Emma, I'm so glad you're here with me. I've come to love you in these past few weeks."

Emma's heart warmed at Ruth's words, her fears momentarily forgotten. "Ruth, you're very dear to me, too," Emma admitted. "And it's not just because I work here. I genuinely enjoy your company. You're a kind soul."

A blush spread across Ruth's pale cheeks as she dipped her head, giggling. "I can't believe I just said that. I sound so sappy!"

Emma laughed along with her, shaking her head. "Oh Ruth, you're a breath of fresh air in this huge manor," she said. "You're allowed to be a little sappy every now and then."

Their laughter echoed in the quiet room, the two women sharing a moment of genuine camaraderie and friendship. Emma cherished these moments, holding on to them like precious gems.

After all, she did not know how long she would be allowed to experience such joy. Emma pushed those thoughts away, determined to focus on the present. Right now, all that mattered was Ruth's well-being, and Emma's newfound happiness.

***

Emma carried the tray of empty dishes down to the kitchen. The scent of fresh bread wafted from the oven, making her mouth water. Cook, a rotund, cherub-faced woman, turned from the stove with a welcoming grin.

"Ah, Miss Emma," she greeted, her voice as warm as the kitchen hearth. "How is Miss Ruth today?"

"She's doing well, thank you," Emma responded, setting the tray on the kitchen counter. "She even managed to finish her soup."

"Good, good," Cook clapped her hands, beaming. "I've added some extra herbs, heard it helps with the recovery."

"I think it worked, she seemed to have her strength today."

Cook winked, bustling back to the stove. "That's the power of good cooking, my dear. Now, what's on your mind? You've got that worried look."

Emma sighed, biting her lower lip. "It's just... I feel like I'm taking advantage of William and Ruth. Ruth's health has improved, and I can't help but feel... redundant."

Cook's spoon stilled over the pot, and she turned to look at Emma. Her eyes were kind as she spoke. "Emma, listen to me. You are not taking advantage of anyone. Miss Ruth and Master Maxwell are happy to have you here. We all are."

"It's only… I was hired to look after Ruth, and now she doesn't need me, not as much as before."

"You don't only bring assistance, Emma," Cook said, her gaze softening. "You bring joy. To Ruth, to Master Maxwell, and to everyone in this house. You've brought a light to this manor that's been missing for a long time."

"But-"

"No buts, Emma," Cook interjected, wiping her hands on her apron. "The way I see it, you're part of this family now. Miss Ruth adores you, Master Maxwell respects you, and we are all glad to have you. So, no more talk of leaving, all right?"

Emma blinked back tears, touched by Cook's words. "Thank you, Cook," she managed to say, her throat tight with emotion. "I really needed to hear that."

Cook nodded, her kind gaze resting on Emma. "We're a family here, Emma. Families take care of each other. Remember that."

With Cook's comforting words echoing in her ears, Emma walked out of the bustling kitchen. She felt a lightness in her chest, but a shadow of unease still lurked in the corners of her mind. She looked down at her hands,

twisting the plain cotton apron between her
fingers. What was her place here in the grand
manor, among people of wealth and standing?

Cook might say she was family, but did
she truly belong? She was no longer just a
caretaker, but neither was she a guest. She
didn't have a defined place, and that
ambiguity troubled her.

She continued to stroll aimlessly
through the sprawling manor, her mind lost in
a sea of thoughts. Perhaps she could persuade
William to allow her to work as a maid? After
all, she was used to doing household chores
and she wasn't afraid of hard work. But what
if he preferred to see her leave, much like
Edward had done?

Doubts swirled in her mind as she
absentmindedly navigated through the

labyrinth of hallways, her steps silent on the plush carpet. A twinge of bitterness rose within her. Why did she always have to prove her worth? Why couldn't she just have a place to call home?

Lost in her thoughts, she almost didn't realise where she had wandered. She paused in front of a heavy wooden door, its polished surface reflecting the flickering light from the hallway lamps. It was William's study.

She lingered outside, hesitant. She knew it was late and he would likely be inside, poring over papers and books. A part of her yearned to knock on the door and pour out her fears to him, but another part feared his reaction. What if he dismissed her concerns? Worse, what if he agreed that she had overstayed her welcome?

Emma sighed, her shoulders slumping. The last thing she wanted was to become a burden. Her hands tightened around her apron, the fabric crumpling beneath her grip. She had always fought for her place in the world, and she would continue to do so. She would not be cast aside.

With a renewed sense of determination, she took a deep breath and turned away from the study. Tomorrow, she decided, she would speak to William. She would plead her case, and hope for the best. For now, she needed to gather her thoughts and steel her resolve. After all, her future depended on it.

Before Emma could walk away, the study door creaked open, revealing William. His brows arched in surprise upon seeing her, a soft smile warming his face. "Emma, I didn't expect to see you here."

She gave a weak smile in return, her heart pounding in her chest. "I...I was just passing by. Didn't mean to intrude."

"No intrusion at all," William assured, leaning against the door frame. His gaze studied her for a moment, a flicker of something undefined crossing his features. "In fact, I've been meaning to talk to you."

"Really?" Emma found her voice barely above a whisper.

"Yes," William admitted, running a hand through his hair. "I...I find that I've been wishing we could spend more time together."

Emma blinked at him, surprised. "We do spend a lot of time together, William. With Ruth, and sometimes alone too."

"Yes, we do," he agreed, his eyes shining in the lamplight. "I meant time...just you and I. I enjoy our conversations and...your company."

His words sent a flutter through Emma's heart. "I enjoy your company too, William," she confessed, her gaze dropping to the floor. Yet, the ghost of her fears still lingered. "I can't help but feel I've overstayed my welcome here."

"No," William denied instantly, concern knitting his brows together. "Why would you say that, Emma?"

She bit her lip, uncertain if she should reveal her fears. William had always been kind and understanding, especially after their initial misunderstanding. "It's just...Ruth is getting better and I can't help but feel..." She trailed off, a lump forming in her throat.

"Feel what, Emma?" His voice was soft, inviting her to share her fears.

"That once Ruth doesn't need me anymore...I'll be...disposable."

The silence that followed her confession was heavy, broken only by the distant ticking of a clock. She dared to look up, finding William watching her with a strange mix of emotions.

"Emma," he began, his voice firm, "You are not, and never will be, disposable."

He took a step closer, his gaze earnest. "You are a part of this household. You're a part of our lives. Ruth's and mine."

His words washed over Emma like a soothing balm. Would his reassurances last? Only time would tell. Yet for that moment, standing in front of William, her fears seemed a little less daunting.

As William's words continued to echo in Emma's mind, she found herself drawn into his earnest gaze. She was aware of their closeness, their breaths mingling in the quiet space between them. Her heart pounded in her chest, a strange yet alluring mix of fear and anticipation. It felt like they were on the edge of something important, something unspoken.

"William, I..." she began, her voice tremulous.

"Yes, Emma?" he prompted, his gaze flickering between her eyes and her lips.

"I appreciate your kindness, truly I do," she confessed, struggling to keep her voice steady. "But I..."

William cut her off gently, his fingers coming up to delicately brush a stray lock of hair from her face. The intimate gesture sent shivers down her spine. "What is it, Emma?"

She found herself leaning into his touch, her eyelids fluttering shut as a wave of emotion washed over her. She could feel the warmth radiating from his body, the anticipation in the air palpable.

He leaned in, his breath warm against her lips. Just as she thought he would bridge the gap, she snapped her eyes open, backing away abruptly. The confusion in his eyes tore at her heart, but she knew she had to protect herself.

"Emma?" he asked, concern seeping into his voice.

"I can't, William," she blurted out, her hands clasping together nervously. "I mean, I...I should...go."

His brows furrowed in confusion. "I don't understand, Emma. Have I done something wrong?"

"No, no. It's not you, William," she quickly assured him. "It's me."

He looked even more perplexed, "Emma, whatever it is, we can talk about it."

She shook her head, her heart heavy. "It's...I...There's just too much, William. Too much baggage, too many things I haven't sorted through. And I'm afraid that a man like you...a man as good as you...shouldn't have to deal with all of that."

"Emma," he started, but she raised a hand to stop him.

"Please, William," she pleaded, her eyes glistening with unshed tears. "I need to sort myself out. Please...understand."

She barely waited for his nod before fleeing from the room, leaving a stunned and hurt William behind. She didn't want to run away, didn't want to hurt him. She needed to sort through her feelings, her fears. She needed to heal. For her, for Ruth...and for William.

Chapter Sixteen

The gaslights were dimmed, the room awash in soft shadows. William sat on the edge of his bed, a small, velvet box open in his hand. The glow from the solitary candle on the bedside table flickered, casting warm, dancing light onto the precious object nestled within the box.

His mother's wedding ring.

The exquisite band of gold was encrusted with small, glittering diamonds that twinkled in the candlelight, their radiance belying the years they had seen. The ring was more than just an heirloom; it was a symbol of his family's lineage, the love between his parents, and the legacy of commitment that he hoped to pass on.

William found his thoughts wandering back to Emma. To the twinkle in her blue eyes that rivalled the sparkle of the diamonds before him, to the warmth of her smile that shone brighter than any gemstone. He thought of her gentle care of Ruth, her infectious laughter filling the manor, her endearing blush each time their hands accidentally brushed.

He knew he loved her, loved her with an intensity that both thrilled and scared him. He loved her strength, her resilience, her kindness. He loved her spirit, her dedication to Ruth, her ability to find joy even amidst the trials life threw at her.

It was this love that had him holding the family ring, contemplating a proposal. He knew there were obstacles; her apprehension, her doubts, the class differences, the fear that he'd cast her away like her uncle did. He was willing to surmount all these, if only to provide her the security she craved, the love she deserved.

Holding the ring close to his heart, he pictured her delicate fingers adorned with it. He could almost hear her gasp of surprise, see her eyes light up, feel her soft lips on his in a tender kiss of acceptance.

Closing the velvet box with a soft click, he placed it back into the drawer, his heart heavy with anticipation and a tinge of fear. He knew he had a task at hand, a task to reassure Emma, to convince her of his sincerity, to make her understand that his love for her was not a fleeting emotion, but a lasting promise.

In the quiet of his room, he made a solemn vow. He would prove to her that his love was genuine, that his intentions were honourable. He would show her that he saw beyond the class, beyond the past tragedies, beyond the exterior, and into her heart, which he found more precious than any family heirloom.

When the time was right, he would ask her to be his wife. The woman he wished to wake up next to every day, the woman he wanted to share his life with, the woman he hoped to build a future with.

***

The crackling fire in Ruth's room did little to temper the excitement that bubbled within William as he confessed his intentions to his younger sister.

"Ruth, I..." he began, glancing nervously at the porcelain teacup in his hands, "I need your advice. It's about Emma."

Ruth's eyes lit up at the mention of her beloved friend. "Yes, William? What about her?" she asked, her voice brimming with curiosity.

"Well," he hesitated, setting his teacup on the tray before him, "I...I intend to propose to her."

The room fell into a deafening silence, broken only by the intermittent pops and crackles from the fireplace. Ruth sat in stunned silence, her hands clasped in her lap, a slow smile spreading across her face. "William," she finally said, her voice barely above a whisper, "That's wonderful news! I cannot think of anyone more perfect for you."

"Ruth, do you think she will accept? I don't want to presume..." William's voice trailed off, his concern palpable.

Ruth chuckled, her laughter like a sweet melody. "William, you really are quite dense at times. Do you not see how she looks at you? How she talks about you? I am certain she feels the same way about you."

"She...she talks about me?" William asked, his heart skipping a beat. He felt a warmth flood his chest at the thought of Emma speaking of him with fondness.

"Yes, William. Emma talks of you with such affection, such love. She has confessed as much to me. Like you, she fears the consequences. She fears the potential rejection," Ruth confided.

Hope bloomed in William's chest. He was not presuming. Emma did share his feelings, even if she kept them hidden behind a veil of apprehension. "I need to reassure her, Ruth. I need her to know that my intentions are pure, that my love for her is unending."

"I think a proposal would be quite convincing, William," Ruth teased, her eyes sparkling with delight.

"You're right. I've decided. I'll propose tonight. I'll arrange for a private dinner for the two of us, and ask her then," he resolved, the knot of anxiety in his stomach uncoiling slightly at his sister's reassurance.

"Oh, William!" Ruth exclaimed, clapping her hands together in joy, "I am so excited for you both. I know Emma will say yes."

"If she doesn't?" he asked, the worry creeping back into his voice.

Ruth held her brother's hand in hers, squeezing gently. "Then, dear brother, you fight. Fight for her, for the love you both share. Do not let fear or doubt win."

William nodded, feeling bolstered by Ruth's words. He would propose to Emma that night, and he would fight for their love, no matter what.

William walked out of Ruth's room, feeling a wave of new-found confidence wash over him. He made his way down the grand staircase, his steps echoing through the quiet halls, each one bringing him closer to his destination - the bustling heart of the house, the kitchen.

Cook, a robust woman with kind eyes and rosy cheeks, was humming a lively tune as she stirred a pot of stew. She looked up as he entered, her smile broadening as she saw him.

"Well now, Master Maxwell! To what do I owe this visit?" she asked, wiping her hands on her apron.

"Cook," he began, taking a deep breath, "I need a favour."

She tilted her head, her eyebrows knitting together in curiosity. "A favour, sir? Whatever you need, just say the word."

"I'm planning to have a private dinner tonight," he stated, "with Miss Emma."

The moment the words left his mouth, Cook's eyes sparkled with understanding. She let out a hearty laugh, clapping her hands together. "Oh! I knew this day would come. You're going to propose to our dear Emma, aren't you?"

William blinked in surprise, then let out a chuckle. "Is it really that obvious, Cook?"

"Clear as a bell, sir!" Cook said, her laughter filling the kitchen. "Don't you worry, I'll prepare a special meal for the occasion. A private, romantic dinner for two. How about roast duck with a side of mashed potatoes and green beans, followed by a sweet, decadent chocolate cake for dessert?"

"That sounds wonderful, Cook. Thank you," he said, feeling a wave of relief wash over him. "It needs to be perfect. I...I need it to be perfect."

"And it will be, Master Maxwell. Emma is a wonderful girl, and she cares for you deeply. I have seen it in the way she looks at you when she thinks no one is watching," Cook confided, her voice softening.

"Yes, I've heard," William replied, a hint of a smile tugging at his lips. "Ruth told me as much."

"Then you have nothing to worry about, sir," Cook said with an encouraging smile. "Just speak from the heart, and I'm certain she will say yes."

"I hope you're right, Cook," he said, his heart pounding in his chest. "Thank you, for everything."

"No need for thanks, sir. I just want to see you both happy," Cook replied, giving him a warm, motherly smile. "Now, off you go. I have a dinner to prepare."

With a grateful nod, William turned to leave, his heart filled with a mixture of hope and anxiety. But amidst all the uncertainty, one thing was clear - he was going to propose to Emma, and he would do everything in his power to ensure she said yes.

William found himself pausing at the end of the hall, taking a moment to lean against the cool marble wall. He took in deep, calming breaths, his heart pounding like a drummer's beat. He was about to propose to Emma, the woman who had so quickly found her way into his heart. The weight of the decision was nearly overwhelming.

He pushed himself off the wall and made his way towards his room, his footsteps echoing ominously in the empty hallway. Each step was heavy, as if he were walking against the tide, yet there was a determined rhythm to his pace. This was a step he needed to take, a risk worth taking.

Once in his room, he opened the top drawer of his dresser and pulled out a small velvet box. He paused, staring at the box for a long moment before opening it. The ring nestled inside was as beautiful as ever, a testament to his late mother's timeless elegance.

The sight of the ring brought forth a flurry of emotions. He felt a rush of nostalgia, remembering his mother's radiant smile every time she wore the ring. Then came a pang of sadness, for he wished she could be here to meet Emma, to share in his joy.

And finally, anxiety clawed at his heart. The ring was a symbol of his love and commitment, a love he hoped Emma reciprocated. He knew she cared for him, he could see it in her warm smiles and hear it in her soft laughter. Did she truly love him as Ruth and Cook seemed to think she did?

He picked up the ring, feeling the cool metal against his fingers, the diamond catching the light and scattering it in a colourful dance. It was the perfect ring for Emma, as radiant and captivating as she was.

He closed the box and tucked it into his pocket, then moved towards the mirror. His reflection stared back at him, a man on the verge of proposing, filled with hope and riddled with doubts. He straightened his jacket and smoothed down his hair, forcing a confident smile.

"Emma," he said to his reflection, "I love you. Will you marry me?"

The words hung heavy in the air, a silent witness to his resolution. He sighed, his gaze lingering on his reflection. He wasn't sure if he was ready, if he could face potential rejection. But one thing was clear - he loved Emma. He was willing to take the risk, for a chance at a life with her.

With one last nod at his reflection, he turned away from the mirror, the ring weighing heavy in his pocket. A cocktail of hope and apprehension coursed through his veins as he stepped out of his room, the echoes of his proposal lingering behind him.

Tonight, he would ask Emma to be his wife. No matter what her response was, he knew he would cherish her, always.

Chapter Seventeen

The sight of William, seated alone at the elegantly set dining table, took Emma's breath away. A beautiful array of dishes were laid out before him, a feast fit for a king. Her heart skipped a beat at the sight of her favourite buttered vegetables arranged elegantly among the array of sumptuous dishes. His efforts touched her, a symbol of the consideration he showed her always.

"Where is Ruth?" Emma asked, her eyes darting around the room in search of her dear friend. She was met only by the soft glow of candlelight flickering in the otherwise empty room.

William looked up at her, a hint of nervousness crossing his usually confident eyes. "Ruth... Ruth won't be joining us tonight. I wanted to spend the evening alone with you, Emma."

His words sent a jolt through her, making her heart flutter erratically. Alone with William... A rush of excitement swirled within her, a maelstrom of anticipation, surprise, and a speck of fear.

They settled into their seats, the heavy silence of the room punctuated only by the soft clinking of cutlery against porcelain. William appeared tense, a stark contrast to his usual composed demeanour. His gaze held a certain intensity, his green eyes shimmering with an emotion she dared not name.

He reached into his pocket and pulled out a small box, which he held in the palm of his trembling hand. The sight of the ring box filled her with a sense of dread and elation. A surge of emotions whirled through her, rendering her speechless. Was this... Could it be...?

The room suddenly felt too small, the air too thin. She watched him, frozen in disbelief, as he opened the box to reveal a magnificent ring. The beautiful piece of jewellery twinkled under the soft candlelight, an emblem of love and commitment. It was a moment she had only dreamt of, and yet, here it was, unfolding before her.

Under the soft glow of the candlelight, William swallowed hard, a rush of emotions reflected in his brilliant green eyes. His gaze bore into Emma's, revealing a raw vulnerability she'd never seen before.

"Emma," he began, his voice slightly shaky, "I must confess, there are things about me that you know better than anyone else, and yet, there are corners of my heart that only you've managed to illuminate."

He took a deep breath, his eyes never leaving hers. "From the moment I first saw you, I was drawn to your spirit, your courage, and the unyielding strength with which you faced every challenge life has thrown at you. You've experienced hardships that no one should, and yet, you continue to bloom, ever resilient and beautiful."

He paused, his gaze softened. "I know you worry about belonging. I know you fear that happiness might slip away as swiftly as it comes. I want you to know that I've come to love you, Emma, not despite your past but because of it. You are the strongest, bravest woman I've ever known, and I consider myself fortunate to have met you."

Tears welled in Emma's eyes, her heart pounding in her chest. She looked at the man in front of her, offering her not just a ring, but a promise of a future filled with love and security. A future she'd only dreamt of.

"I want to make you happy," he said, his voice barely a whisper. "I want to give you the love and the life you deserve, a life that's as beautiful as you are. I want us to build a home, not just a house, filled with laughter, shared dreams, and, above all, love. I want to stand by you, through the good times and the bad, to hold your hand and to cherish you for the rest of my life."

With that, William held up the ring. "Emma, will you do me the honour of becoming my wife?"

His heartfelt proposal hung in the air, an offer of love and companionship, of shared dreams and a lifetime of togetherness. Emma felt the tears slip down her cheeks as she looked into William's hopeful eyes. Her past was filled with heartache and struggle, but here was a chance for happiness, for love, and most importantly, for a home. A chance to be loved and cherished for who she was, by a man who saw her worth, her strength, and her heart. And in that moment, amidst the fear and uncertainty, she knew her answer.

With a nod and a choked whisper, she replied, "Yes, William. Yes, I'll marry you."

As Emma's whispered "yes" filled the room, the relief that washed over William's face was evident. He reached out, cradling her face in his hands, and in the dim candlelight, she could see the love and adoration in his eyes. It was mirrored by her own feelings, a vast and unexplored ocean of emotions that she had for him.

He moved closer, his gaze dropping to her lips before meeting her eyes again, silently asking for her permission. With a small nod, she granted it, and as their lips met, it was as though a dam had burst within her. Every barrier, every ounce of fear and uncertainty she'd held back came crashing down in the face of this overwhelming love she felt for the man before her.

Their first kiss was a gentle exploration, as soft as the flutter of a butterfly's wings, as intimate as the whispered confession of a shared secret. She clung to him, her hands finding solace in the fabric of his dinner jacket as she lost herself in the sweet promise of their kiss.

The kiss deepened, a crescendo of shared desires and unspoken confessions, the final breaking down of walls between two hearts that had learned to love amidst the rubble of their pasts. William pulled back, his forehead resting against hers, and the silence that followed was heavy with words left unsaid. His thumb traced the contour of her lips, still tingling from their first shared kiss.

"I love you, Emma," he whispered, a tremor in his voice. "I've loved you since the moment I saw you."

Tears glistened in Emma's eyes, her heart overwhelmed with the sheer intensity of her emotions. She clung to him, her arms wrapping around his neck as she leaned into him. His confession was met with her own, whispered into the quiet space between them.

"I love you too, William," she admitted, her voice barely audible. "I didn't think it was possible to feel this way, to love this deeply, but you've shown me it's possible."

He smiled, a beautiful, heartfelt smile that made her heart flutter. Slipping the ring onto her finger, he brought her hand up to his lips, pressing a gentle kiss to the back of her hand. The ring felt heavy, a tangible promise of the love and life they would share.

As they sat there, their hands intertwined and their hearts beating in sync, Emma couldn't help but marvel at the journey she had embarked upon. From the pain of her past, she had found hope, and in William, she had found love.

As they shifted back into their seats, the delicious spread before them seemed to radiate an added charm. Laughter and mirth filled the room, bouncing off the richly papered walls, creating a cocoon of happiness that enveloped them.

"I can't believe I'm going to be Mrs William Maxwell," Emma laughed, her eyes sparkling with happiness.

William grinned at her, reaching over to take her hand, the engagement ring sparkling in the dim light. "I can't believe I'm lucky enough to have you as my wife."

They began to eat, the food tasting better than anything Emma had ever had before. Not because it was especially delicious, although Cook had outdone herself, but because every bite was shared in the bliss of their engagement.

During dinner, their conversation flowed easily. They discussed the various things they would like to do in the future – the places they wanted to visit, the books they wanted to read together, the life they were eager to build. Emma felt giddy with the reality of it all, a constant smile playing on her lips.

At one point, William leaned back in his chair, a thoughtful expression on his face. "Emma," he began, a certain hesitancy in his voice, "Would you like to have an engagement party in the New Year?"

She looked at him in surprise, before a soft smile graced her lips. The idea of a lavish party, of her in a gorgeous dress surrounded by people who wished her well, was overwhelming. Although, it was part of this new life she was embarking upon, a life of comfort, happiness, and love.

"I'd love that, William," she replied, squeezing his hand in reassurance. "It would be wonderful."

His face broke into a relieved smile. "I'm glad," he said, and it was easy to see the relief in his eyes. "I want you to feel welcomed and loved, not just by me, but by everyone who's important to us."

Tears welled in Emma's eyes at his words. She had never felt so cherished, so important to someone before. It was an intoxicating feeling, and she found herself caught up in the beauty of it all.

"I feel loved, William," she said sincerely, her hand reaching across the table to squeeze his. "You've given me a place to call home, a family. It's more than I ever dreamed of."

His hand covered hers, his thumb stroking her knuckles softly. "You deserve all of it, Emma. And I promise to spend the rest of my life making sure you never doubt that."

As dinner wound down, they lingered at the table, in no rush to break the magical spell that the evening had woven around them. They talked and laughed, shared hopes and dreams, and simply revelled in the intimacy of the moment. The world outside seemed to recede, leaving only them and the bubble of their shared joy.

"William," Emma said at last, her voice hushed as if she were sharing a secret. "I never thought... I never dared to hope that something like this could happen to me. To be loved, to be cherished... it's more than I ever dreamed of."

William reached out to cover her hand with his, giving it a gentle squeeze. "Emma, you are a remarkable woman," he told her earnestly. "You are deserving of all the love and happiness in the world."

Their eyes met, and in his gaze, Emma saw reflected all the love and affection she felt for him. It filled her with a warm glow, spreading through her chest until she felt like she might burst from the sheer happiness.

Finally, they rose from the table, their hands entwined. As they moved towards the door, Emma turned to him. "I have something to tell you," she said, her heart hammering in her chest.

"What is it?" he asked, his brow furrowing in concern.

Taking a deep breath, she met his gaze. "Your proposal... it was perfect. And I... I am happier than I have ever been."

Her confession hung in the air, raw and vulnerable. William looked at her for a moment, and then his face broke into a wide grin. "I am too, Emma. Happier than I ever thought possible."

His words washed over her, soothing any lingering fears or doubts. She stepped into his embrace, her arms wrapping around his waist. He responded immediately, pulling her closer and pressing a soft kiss to her forehead. Emma closed her eyes, relishing the feel of his arms around her, the warm solidity of him.

As they pulled away, William cupped her face, his thumb gently wiping away a stray tear that had slipped down her cheek. He bent down and kissed her, a sweet, chaste kiss that nevertheless sent shivers down her spine. When they broke apart, she was breathless, her heart beating wildly in her chest.

In that moment, she knew. This was where she was meant to be, with William, by his side. This was the happiness she had been yearning for all her life, and she was finally home.

"Thank you, William," she whispered, pressing her forehead against his. "For everything."

As they stood there, embraced in the soft candlelight, the world outside seemed to fade away, leaving only the two of them and their shared love. A promise of a new beginning, a brighter future, and a love that was destined to last a lifetime.

Chapter Eighteen

That next morning found them all gathered in the drawing room, a soft morning light spilling in through the large windows. Emma felt a flutter of nerves in her stomach as she and William entered the room together, his hand firmly around hers.

Ruth was already there, perched on the sofa next to Cook, her frail body wrapped in a warm shawl. The footman, a humble man by the name of Harold, stood respectfully by the door.

"Good morning, everyone," William greeted, his voice firm yet full of warmth. He squeezed Emma's hand reassuringly, and she drew strength from his presence. They had something important to share, something wonderful, and she couldn't wait to see the joy on their friends' faces.

"We have an announcement to make," William said, his gaze meeting Emma's. A shared smile passed between them, and she could feel her cheeks warming under his affectionate gaze.

Ruth, with her youthful curiosity, was the first to respond. "Oh? What is it?" she asked, her eyes wide with anticipation.

It was Emma who answered. Taking a deep breath, she lifted her hand, showing them the ring that William had presented to her just the previous night. "William has asked me to marry him, and I have said yes," she said, her voice ringing with joy.

A stunned silence followed her announcement, then the room erupted into a chorus of delighted exclamations. Ruth squealed in joy, her hands flying to her mouth, and Cook clapped her hands together, her eyes misting over with emotion. Even their footman, Harold, always the picture of decorum, couldn't suppress his wide smile.

"Oh, Emma!" Ruth cried, throwing her arms around her older friend, "I'm so happy for you!"

"Congratulations, both of you!" Cook chimed in, wiping at her eyes with a corner of her apron. "You'll make a lovely couple, I just know it."

Harold, too, offered his sincere congratulations, a genuine warmth in his eyes.

"Very happy for you, sir, Miss Emma," he said, nodding respectfully at both of them.

Laughter filled the drawing room as they sat around sharing stories, congratulations, and wishes of happiness. Cook told funny tales of past engagements and weddings in the family, her anecdotes filling the room with warmth. Harold, more reserved but equally jovial, shared his best wishes and his belief in their perfect match.

In between shared glances and secret smiles, William and Emma listened to the stories, their hands intertwined. The air was alight with joy and anticipation, the scent of happiness thick in the room. It felt as if every part of the room, every piece of the manor, was sharing in their joy.

"Almost Christmas, too," Cook commented, her cheeks rosy from laughter. "What a wonderful gift for us all!" She grinned, her eyes twinkling. "There's no better time for love than at Christmas."

Everyone agreed, the festive spirit only adding to their excitement. The chandelier above their heads twinkled brightly, reflecting the pure joy in the room. The Christmas tree in the corner stood tall and proud, its ornaments glinting under the warm glow of the room. It was a beautiful scene, something straight out of a painting.

"Speaking of Christmas," Ruth chimed in, her pale face aglow with happiness. "Emma, you must help me choose a dress for Christmas Eve!" She looked at Emma with pleading eyes. "Please say you will."

"Of course, Ruth," Emma agreed, her heart swelling at the girl's request. The bond they shared was as strong as ever, and she knew it would only grow stronger.

Everyone continued to chat, the conversation flowing effortlessly. Emma and William often found themselves lost in their own little world, sharing whispered words and stolen glances. During one such moment, when everyone else was occupied with their own conversations, William leaned in, capturing Emma's lips in a sweet, chaste kiss.

The world seemed to still for a moment, everything else fading into the background. Their connection was electric, a spark that lit up their little corner of the room. Emma felt a rush of emotion, her heart swelling with a love so strong, it took her breath away.

They broke apart slowly, their smiles matching the radiant happiness in their eyes. Their secret kiss had gone unnoticed, or so it seemed, but the love between them was far from hidden. It was palpable, a force that filled the room and wrapped them all in its warm embrace.

Cook's voice sliced through their blissful bubble, her jovial laugh ringing through the drawing room. "Oh, I couldn't be happier for you both!" She wiped a tear from her cheek, her face beaming. "Just look at you two!"

Emma and William turned their attention back to the group, their hands slipping apart as they shared amused glances.

"Thank you, Cook," Emma said, her heart still fluttering from the kiss.

"Yes, we are truly grateful for your kind words and good wishes," William added, his gaze never straying far from Emma. His hand found hers under the table, giving it a gentle squeeze.

After a few more minutes of chatter and well wishes, William turned to Emma, leaning in to whisper in her ear. "Shall we steal a moment for ourselves?"

"Thought you'd never ask," Emma whispered back, her lips curving into a smile.

"Excuse us," William addressed the room, standing and offering his hand to Emma. "We'd like a moment alone to... gather our thoughts."

The group sent them off with understanding smiles, Cook's eyes twinkling with mischief. "Of course, of course," she said, waving them away with a hand. "We'll get back to work."

As they left the room, Emma could hardly suppress her laughter. She had never been happier. As they moved through the corridors of the manor, their hands remained linked, their hearts beating as one.

They ended up in William's study, the door closing behind them with a soft click. The room was bathed in the warm glow of the fire, the dancing flames casting flickering shadows on the walls. A sense of peace settled over them, the noise and excitement from the drawing room a distant memory.

William turned to Emma, his hand coming up to caress her face. "Are you happy, Emma?" he asked, his voice soft, his eyes reflecting the firelight.

She looked up at him, her heart feeling full to the brim. "I have never been happier, William," she confessed, reaching up to cover his hand with hers. "It's overwhelming... in a good way."

"I know," he said, his thumb brushing her cheek. "It's a lot to take in." He pulled her close, their foreheads touching. "Just know that I'm excited to spend the rest of my life with you."

"Yes," she agreed, her voice barely above a whisper. "And I, you."

The warmth of the study wrapped around them like a soft blanket, the only sounds the crackling fire and their steady breaths. They stood together, hands intertwined, their shared happiness a palpable energy in the room. It was a quiet, intimate moment, offering them a chance to process the day's whirlwind of emotions.

Emma looked into William's eyes, her heart overflowing with a love she never thought she'd experience. Yet here she was, basking in it, soaking in the tranquillity of their shared solitude. The weight of her engagement ring was a constant reminder of the beautiful promise they'd made to each other, a symbol of a future that looked brighter with every passing moment.

"I wish my parents could have seen this, William," she confessed softly, breaking the comfortable silence. "I know they would have been so happy for us."

William squeezed her hands gently, giving her a reassuring smile. "I'm sure they are, Emma," he replied. "They're watching over you, and they're undoubtedly proud of the woman you've become."

A small smile pulled at her lips as she allowed his words to comfort her. She pictured her parents, their faces a blur of fading memories, looking down on her from a place of peace and love. She could almost hear their laughter, see their smiles. It was a comforting thought.

"Do you think they'd like me?" William asked, breaking into her thoughts. She looked at him, surprised by the question. His eyes were full of genuine curiosity, his expression earnest.

"Of course, they would," she answered without hesitation. "You are kind, generous, and you love me. They would have adored you, William."

He looked relieved, his smile returning in full force. "I'm glad," he murmured, pulling her closer. "I love you, Emma. I want to do everything I can to make you happy, to give you the life you deserve."

Emma's heart swelled, her eyes glistening with unshed tears. "You already do, William," she said, her voice choked with emotion. "I'm here, with you. I can't think of anything that would make me happier."

As she leaned into him, their hearts beating in sync, she knew she was home. She had found love in the most unexpected place, and now, it was a love that promised to stay, to grow. As she imagined her parents, looking down on her with joy, she knew she had made the right choice. She was where she was meant to be. She was home.

As they left the comforting embrace of the study, the scent of a still-burning fire and the faint echo of shared laughter followed them. Emma nestled herself against William's side, her heart thrumming in time with his.

"I'm looking forward to Christmas," she said, her voice brimming with anticipation. "I can already tell it's going to be the best one ever."

William glanced down at her, a look of pure adoration on his face. "I'm going to make sure it is," he promised, his voice steady and determined.

The soft glow of the drawing room light guided them back towards the others. As they re-entered, they found the room still buzzing with cheerful chatter, the Christmas tree twinkling in the corner. Their friends' laughter filled the room, but their eyes were drawn to Ruth, slumped in her chair, sleeping peacefully.

William and Emma exchanged a quiet smile, their hearts filled with a contentment that spoke volumes. As they looked upon Ruth's peaceful face, they realised that this was their family. This manor, these people, this was where they belonged.

Emma's heart swelled with a happiness she'd never thought possible. Despite the hardships she'd faced, she was here, standing beside the man she loved, surrounded by friends who were more like family. It was more than she ever could have imagined, and she was grateful for every single moment.

Embracing William's arm a bit tighter, she rested her head against his shoulder. Their shared silence was comfortable, filled with mutual understanding and love. This was her family, and she loved them more than anything else in the world.

Life had dealt her a challenging hand, but standing there in that moment, Emma wouldn't have changed a thing. Her heart was full, her spirit was at peace, and she had an incredibly bright future to look forward to.

As the evening wore on, the couple returned to the happy chatter around them, their hearts echoing the festive cheer of the room. As they laughed and talked, Emma felt an overwhelming sense of belonging. She was home, truly and completely, in every sense of the word.

As the night drew to a close, the reality of her new life started to set in. No longer an orphan, no longer alone, she was a part of something special. She was a part of a family, a part of a love story she never thought she'd be lucky enough to live.

For the first time in her life, Emma was looking forward to a future filled with love, happiness, and endless possibilities. The knowledge that this would be the best Christmas ever was just the icing on the cake.

As she looked around the room, her heart filled with love for her new family, she couldn't help but smile. This was her happily ever after.

Epilogue

One year later

A year later, the warmth and merriment of Christmas filled the grand manor. This year, the house was even more boisterous with the arrival of William's extended family and their joint friends. The once spacious manor felt positively buzzing with activity. Emma, now the woman of the house, was at the centre of it all.

As she walked through the bustling hallways, she was aware of the eyes following her. It wasn't that they were unwelcoming – quite the opposite. The staff admired her, treated her with respect, and in turn, she had come to care for them deeply. Yet, there was an element of uncertainty, a tiny doubt that lingered in the back of her mind about her ability to oversee such a large household.

She pushed the thought aside as she passed through the kitchen, the aroma of gingerbread and mulled wine wafting into the hallway. Cook, in the thick of preparations, greeted her with a warm smile.

"Good evening, Mrs Emma," she said, dusting her hands on her apron.

"Good evening, Cook," Emma replied, her gaze drifting over the flurry of activity around them. "How are things progressing?"

"As well as can be expected" Cook said with a twinkle in her eye. "A little hectic, but 'tis the season, after all."

Emma laughed, the sound echoing through the busy kitchen. "Indeed, it is." She glanced at the clock, her expression becoming serious. "You've all been working so hard. Please, don't forget to retire early tonight. Spend time with your own families. We wouldn't be where we are without all of you."

Cook's face softened, her eyes reflecting the affection she held for the young woman. "Thank you, Mrs Emma. You're too kind."

Emma left the kitchen, her heart filled with warmth despite the winter chill outside. She moved through the manor, reminding everyone of her request. The housekeepers, footmen, and even the stable hands greeted her warmly, their smiles a testament to the fondness they held for her.

As the day turned into evening, the manor gradually quieted down. The staff trickled out, leaving for their own homes, their faces alight with the promise of spending Christmas with their families. Emma felt a rush of satisfaction, the feeling of a job well done.

Emma thanked the remaining staff members, reminding them of the importance of their own celebrations, before finally escaping the hustle and bustle of the kitchen. She found herself in the drawing room where William was deep in conversation with Ruth, their voices blending into the soft crackling of the fire.

Seeing them together, she felt a wave of affection. Ruth, now the picture of health, had not only regained her strength but also found love in the form of a young gentleman from the neighbouring estate. Their relationship was still in the early stages, but the change in Ruth was apparent.

Upon her arrival, William looked up, his face brightening. "There she is," he said, standing up to greet her. "My beautiful wife."

She laughed, stepping into his arms. "Here I thought you'd be bored of me."

"Impossible," he replied, leaning down to capture her lips in a tender kiss. Their moment was interrupted by a mock gag from Ruth.

"Oh, do spare me the display of affection," she said, but her teasing grin gave away her true feelings. She was just as happy for them as they were for her.

William only laughed, wrapping his arm around Emma's waist as he guided her to the plush armchair. "Emma, you've been running about all day," he said, his tone growing serious. "You must remember to take care of yourself."

Emma rolled her eyes playfully but nodded, realising the truth in his words. She had been so preoccupied with making everyone else's Christmas perfect that she'd barely had a moment's rest.

"You're right," she admitted, leaning into his side. "I suppose I'm just eager for everyone to enjoy the holiday."

His thumb traced gentle circles on her hand, the touch reassuring. "We will," he assured her. "Thanks to your incredible efforts. Don't forget, this is your Christmas too. We want you to enjoy it as well."

Ruth nodded in agreement, adding her voice to the conversation. "Emma, you've done so much for this household. Please, take some time for yourself."

Emma felt a warmth spreading through her chest, a combination of gratitude and love for her new family. She leaned her head onto William's shoulder, a content sigh escaping her lips. "All right," she said, glancing up at William with a playful glint in her eyes. "Only if you promise to help with the leftovers tomorrow."

He chuckled, pressing a soft kiss to her forehead. "Anything for you, my love. We're a team, after all."

With Ruth's laughter filling the room, the fire casting a warm glow around them, and William's arm around her shoulder, Emma couldn't help but feel overwhelmed by happiness. This was her family, her home, and her Christmas. It was more than she had ever dreamed of, and she was ready to embrace it fully.

***

Christmas morning dawned with a quiet hush, a serene silence in the midst of the joyful chaos that had surrounded the mansion over the past few days. Emma sat in the grand drawing room, a beautifully wrapped gift from William in her lap. The twinkling Christmas tree lights danced in her eyes as she carefully lifted the lid.

Inside was a breath-taking brooch, crafted from gold and studded with emeralds, her birthstone. In the shape of a butterfly, it held a symbolic meaning that did not escape her; she felt her heart swell with the significance of it.

"Oh, William," she murmured, her voice wavering with emotion. She raised her gaze to meet her husband's, a tear trickling down her cheek. "It's beautiful. Thank you."

His smile was wide and filled with a quiet contentment. "You've brought so much change and happiness into our lives, Emma. It seemed fitting."

A bubble of warmth enveloped her as she turned to hand William his gift, her fingers gently nudging the small package towards him. His eyes widened slightly at the sight of the gold pocket watch she'd chosen. The front was etched with intricate designs, and upon opening it, he discovered the inscription: 'Time is eternal with you.'

His eyes met hers, mirroring the love she felt in her heart. His strong arms pulled her into a loving embrace, and his whispered "Thank you, love" brought tears of happiness to her eyes.

Ruth, who had been observing the couple with a knowing smile, received a gift from Emma too. She opened it to reveal a stunning hand-painted porcelain box for her treasured trinkets. Ruth's response - a warm embrace - warmed Emma even more.

William, in turn, presented Ruth with a collection of illustrated poetry books by her favourite author, a touching reminder of their sibling bond. Emma watched as Ruth thanked him, her eyes filled with the love and affection that defined their relationship.

The morning passed with shared laughter and heartfelt words, the joy of the season encasing the room in a warm embrace. Each gift was a testament to their deep understanding of each other. It was in these moments that Emma truly felt a part of this family, more so than ever before.

As the sun began to fill the room with a golden glow, they moved to the dining room for a hearty Christmas breakfast. As they sat around the table, enjoying the warmth of the fire and each other's company, Emma felt an overwhelming sense of belonging. She was part of this family, loved and cherished, and she couldn't have asked for a more beautiful Christmas morning.

As the breakfast dishes were cleared away, the conversation continued, filled with laughter and teasing remarks. The fire crackled in the background, casting a warm, inviting glow throughout the room. Emma found herself caught up in the love that was so palpable within this family.

"To think that only a year ago, I was terrified of the prospect of a Christmas in this house," Emma said with a laugh, the memory feeling distant now. "Now, here I am, happier than I've ever been."

"We are the ones who are truly blessed, Emma," William interjected, his voice filled with sincerity. "Your presence in this house has brought a joy that we could not have imagined. Speaking for myself, I am eternally grateful for your 'yes' that night. Marrying you was the best decision I've ever made."

Ruth chimed in, her eyes sparkling, "I second that! You may have started as my companion, Emma, but you quickly became my friend and now my sister; and not just because you married William," she added teasingly, causing them all to laugh.

Emma's smile softened as she listened to their words, feeling a lump form in her throat. "I often wonder if I'm fit for this lavish life," she confessed quietly. "It's all so different from what I was used to."

William reached over and gently took her hand in his, giving it a comforting squeeze. "Emma, you are more than fit for this life. You are part of this family. You are loved and cherished by every person in this house, not because of any role you play, but because you are you. Your kindness, your strength, your love... That is what makes you fit for this life."

Ruth nodded, echoing her brother's sentiments, "It's not about the wealth or the lavishness, Emma. It's about the love and the bond we all share. You've taught us that, more than anything else."

The room fell silent for a moment, the sincerity of their words hanging in the air. Emma felt a profound sense of love and gratitude well up inside her. Tears pricked at her eyes, but she brushed them away quickly, not wanting to dampen the joy of the morning.

"I love you both," she said simply, her voice choked with emotion. The smiles she received in return were all she needed to know. This was her home. This was her family. She was exactly where she was meant to be.

Emma could hardly contain the wave of emotion that washed over her as she looked between William and Ruth. Her family. How did she get so lucky?

"I love you both too," William responded, his voice thick with emotion. He reached for Ruth's hand and gave it a gentle squeeze.

"Yes, I couldn't have said it better myself," Ruth added, a bright smile spreading across her face. "And you must remember,

Emma. No matter what happens, you'll always be a part of this family."

Emma felt her eyes well up, and she quickly brushed a tear away. "Thank you," she said, her voice barely above a whisper. "Thank you for everything."

"Thank you, Emma, for being you," William replied, pulling her into a gentle hug.

As they embraced, Emma felt a sense of contentment like no other. This was her family. This was her home. No matter where life would take them, she knew she was exactly where she was meant to be.

Their laughter echoed throughout the house, filling the hallways with warmth and love. The scent of pine from the Christmas tree mingled with the lingering aroma of breakfast, creating a sense of homeliness that she hadn't known she had been missing.

Christmas morning transitioned into a delightful afternoon, with playful banter and shared memories, forming new ones that Emma knew she would cherish forever.

As the sun set, painting the sky with hues of gold and crimson, Emma found herself leaning into William, their hands entwined. Ruth was contentedly dozing in her chair, a small smile playing on her lips.

"Here's to our family," William whispered, pressing a tender kiss to Emma's forehead. "And to many more Christmas mornings just like this one."

Emma smiled up at him, her heart full. "To our family," she echoed. "To a lifetime of love."

With that, they welcomed the evening, ready to embrace whatever the future held for them, knowing they would face it together, as a family. They knew that they had a lifetime of joy, laughter, and love to look forward to, and they were ready to cherish every moment.

In that moment, Emma knew that she had found her forever home. This was her happily ever after.

Printed in Great Britain
by Amazon